CW01499413

Have Your Cum ˌ

It's 1981, and two Mormon missionaries randomly assigned to work together as "companions" in Napoli find themselves in trouble. They're falling in love, but the Church forbids gay relationships. As missionaries, they can't date anyone at all, much less other men. If they're found out, they'll be excommunicated, sent home in disgrace, and cast out from their families.

In the aftermath of a devastating earthquake, against a backdrop of poverty and repressive mission culture, Elders Grant and Mortensen knock on doors, endure violent assaults, and face the ultimate challenge—will they be crushed by dedication to their beliefs or will love provide a way for them to escape?

Praise for Johnny Townsend

In *Zombies for Jesus*, "Townsend isn't writing satire, but deeply emotional and revealing portraits of people who are, with a few exceptions, quite lovable."

Kel Munger, *Sacramento News and Review*

In *Sex among the Saints*, "Townsend writes with a deadpan wit and a supple, realistic prose that's full of psychological empathy....he takes his protagonists' moral struggles seriously and invests them with real emotional resonance."

Kirkus Reviews

Let the Faggots Burn: The UpStairs Lounge Fire is "a gripping account of all the horrors that transpired that night, as well as a respectful remembrance of the victims."

Terry Firma, Patheos

"Johnny Townsend's 'Partying with St. Roch' [in the anthology *Latter-Gay Saints*] tells a beautiful, haunting tale."

Kent Brintnall, Out in Print: Queer Book Reviews

Selling the City of Enoch is "sharply intelligent...pleasingly complex...The stories are full of...doubters, but there's no vindictiveness in these pages; the characters continuously poke holes in Mormonism's more extravagant absurdities, but they take very little pleasure in doing so....Many of Townsend's stories...have a provocative edge to them, but this [book] displays a great deal of insight as well...a playful, biting and surprisingly warm collection."

Kirkus Reviews

Gayrabian Nights is "an allegorical tour de force...a hard-core emotional punch."

Gay. Guy. Reading and Friends

The Washing of Brains has "A lovely writing style, and each story [is] full of unique, engaging characters....immensely entertaining."

Rainbow Awards

In *Dead Mankind Walking*, "Townsend writes in an energetic prose that balances crankiness and humor....A rambunctious volume of short, well-crafted essays..."

Kirkus Reviews

Johnny Townsend

Have Your Cum
and Eat It, Too

Johnny Townsend

Cover design by Todd Engel

Special thanks to Donna Banta
and Robert Ramsay
for their editorial assistance

For more of Donna's own work,
please read *Mormon Erotica* and *False Prophet.*

For more of Robert's work,
please read *Restoring the Dream* and *Wreck of the Royal Express*

Contents

Chapter One:

Lovers' Lane, Naples

Even the Bucaneve cookies and a triangle of milk with the other elders hadn't cheered up my companion. Neither did a long shower. After we brushed our teeth, we retired to our room and said our evening companion prayer, in Italian, of course, and then stripped to our garments. Anziano Grant preferred the cotton variety, but I liked the silkier bemberg. The few minutes each day when we walked around in our Mormon underwear was the closest I could ever get to seeing Elder Grant naked. Sometimes, I could see something flopping around in front. Other times, when he leaned over, the slit in the seat would reveal just a little of his crack.

A spaccaculo, if you will.

I'd always found it frustrating, even as a young boy, that Batman didn't wear more form-fitting tights. The Superman movie that came out my senior year of high school wasn't much better. No form-fitting tights for Christopher Reeve, either. Superheroes weren't really brave if they had to hide their bulges.

Elder Grant and I knelt beside our beds and offered individual prayers to "nostro Padre Celeste." Heavenly Father had been human once on another world, which meant he'd sinned at some point before progressing to godhood. It was impossible not to hope he'd liked looking at other men's cracks as well. If he could still eventually reach the Celestial Kingdom, then I could, too.

My companion pulled back the sheet on his cot with a sigh, his eyes looking guiltily in my direction for a split second before turning away. He sat down but didn't slide underneath the covers.

Every time I returned his gaze and he didn't look away, I started hearing Air Supply's "Lost in Love" and had to force myself not to sing along. I'd never understood all those ridiculously sentimental lyrics when the song was released a few months before my mission.

When I'd heard it yesterday during Dual Study, it had taken me a moment to realize the sound was coming from our neighbor's radio.

"Lights Out, I guess," Elder Grant said, giving me a barely perceptible nod. His hair was too dark to be called sandy but too light to be considered brown, too short to move when he bobbed his head.

I walked over to the switch near the bedroom door. It aggravated me that mission rules forbid us from locking that door, or the bathroom door, or the door to the prayer closet where we kept our stock of Church magazines. The zone leaders sometimes popped into any of these rooms without warning, "just to check" on us. Once, Elder Murdock, the senior zone leader here in Napoli 2, had sneaked into our bedroom at 3:00 in the morning and leaned over my bed.

"Are you dreaming worthy dreams?" he shouted. He was trying to be funny. He'd told us over lunch earlier that the mission president didn't want to hear any more elders confessing to masturbation. When I'd frowned in response, he'd teased, "Feeling guilty, Elder? I didn't say it wasn't a sin, just that the prez is tired of hearing about it. I can always keep track of your sins myself."

When Elder Murdock had shouted at me in my sleep, I'd awakened terrorized and then sat up so quickly my head busted his lower lip. He hadn't pulled any more middle of the night inspections, but there was always the possibility he'd try again, perhaps at a slightly less vulnerable distance from my cot.

"Anziano Grant," I said, "I think we need to have Companion Inventory."

He wrinkled his nose. "Now, Anziano Mortensen? It's almost 10:30." He glanced toward the door.

"I'll turn out the lights so they won't know we're up past bedtime." I flicked the switch. Because we'd already lowered the serranda over the window, the room was now pitch black. The lack of even a sliver of light under the door from the hallway revealed the other two companionships had also retired in the last couple of minutes.

I moved slowly over to Elder Grant's cot and sat beside him. The springs creaked unhappily.

"Down at that Lovers' Lane earlier," I said, "you looked so forlorn. I couldn't tell if you were sad for the souls of those people or…"

"You know perfectly well why I was sad." Elder Grant and I had both been out long enough that we enjoyed speaking Italian even when off duty. Of course, so many Italian words were virtually identical to their English equivalent. "Perfettamente" instead of "perfectly" wasn't much of a stretch. After scoring so high on the language aptitude test when I filled out my mission papers the year before, I'd expected to end up in Finland or Taiwan.

Was it too much to hope that Heavenly Father had sent me to the Italy Rome mission expressly to meet Elder Grant?

"Sí," I said. "Lo so." I closed my eyes, though it made no difference in the darkness. My companion had just told me he wanted to share a Cinquecento with me. I felt myself trembling. But if he could be brave, I had to step up, too.

"Do you ever m-masturbate?" I whispered.

I heard a sigh. "You know I do." Of course I knew. Almost every evening immediately after Lights Out, I could hear rustling from my companion's bed, his arm brushing against his sheet loudly as he began beating off. He'd start to moan ever so softly, just loud enough for me to hear but not the other companionship in the next room, or the zone leaders down the hall. When he ejaculated, he'd sigh the tiniest fraction of a decibel more loudly.

I'd wait until I heard him wiping his hand on his sheet before I conducted the exact same performance for him.

But we'd never acknowledged our bedtime activities in any way. When the alarm went off the following morning, Elder Grant's first comment was always, "Another day full of opportunity to serve the Lord."

We'd give our morning companion prayer and then start our day like the missionaries we were.

"Anziano Grant," I continued, shifting on his cot so that our thighs almost touched, and causing the springs to creak once again. I could feel the proximity of my companion's thighs if not their warmth. "Jacking off isn't a terrible sin, is it?"

There was a long silence.

I'd crossed a line and I knew it. Good Mormon boys didn't talk about such things out loud. I started to shift away.

Elder Grant put his hand on my thigh. "No," he said, "it's not." His voice was so weak I could barely hear him. "But what I *want* to do…"

I put my hand on top of his, and we sat on his cot in silence for another few minutes. If this was the most that ever happened between us, it was already the most incredible experience of my life. Better even than baptizing Massimo back in my first district in Quartu.

Nothing could be better than bringing someone into the gospel.

"I wish…" Elder Grant whispered.

Even when I thought of Massimo, I didn't remember him in his suit during his confirmation after the baptism when he was given the gift of the Holy Ghost. I remembered his thirty-year-old figure climbing out of the font with his white clothes clinging tightly to his body.

Thin white clothes.

Too bad Batman never had to be baptized. Or Robin.

"I've got an idea," I said, squeezing my companion's hand. What I was going to suggest was clearly sinful, but I hoped not *too* sinful, perhaps like fantasizing about my Home Teachers back in New Orleans.

"What?" Elder Grant asked immediately. He was from Santa Rosa. Close enough to San Francisco maybe to have a gay person in his ward.

"Sex would be a sin, obviously. We'd be sent back to the States. Excommunicated."

"And your idea?"

"It's not sex if I touch your hand." I squeezed it again. "It's not sex if I touch you on your elbow." I fumbled around for it. "Or your ankle. Or your ear."

Elder Grant made a grunt that wasn't English and wasn't Italian but which still fully conveyed his lack of satisfaction with my idea so far.

"Why don't you stand up?" I suggested. "Face your bed, pull your p-penis out your front slit, and start stroking yourself." I'd looked up the word for "penis" my first month in Sardinia.

"I don't understand."

"I'm going to kneel behind you," I explained, "and pry open your back slit."

"But that—"

"We're not going to have sex," I assured him. "My penis won't get anywhere near you. And I won't touch yours." I hesitated. "I'll just lick your asshole while you masturbate." I switched to English with that last sentence. Breaking a mission rule. My heart started beating faster.

"That's perverted." Elder Grant switched to English as well, even though "pervertito" was an easy word.

"It's just a body part," I said. "It's not a sex organ."

"Can't you lick my elbow?"

"Anziano," I said, "I want to feel intimate with you. As intimate as possible without sinning. If we can't have sex, licking your asshole is the next best way to feel a connection." On the bus on the way home earlier, I'd already made a mental list detailing quite a variety of ways to achieve physical intimacy, but this was what I wanted at that moment.

"I-I'm afraid, Elder Mortensen."

"There's nothing in the scriptures against licking your best friend's asshole."

I stood up and reached for my companion's hands in the dark, pulling him to his feet as well. I turned him away from me and dropped to my knees, tugging at his rear slit. I brushed my face against his cheeks.

"Oh my heck."

"Catch your semen in your hand," I whispered. Then I took a deep breath and pushed my face as deep into his crack as I could, licking everywhere until I found his hole. I could feel my hands on his waist trembling until I heard him groan softly. Then all fear disappeared.

Elder Grant's body began rocking in a manner that let me know he was following my command to beat off.

We weren't having sex. He was masturbating, and I was touching part of his body that wasn't a sex organ.

Of course, a hand wasn't a sex organ, either. I'd fantasized so many times about sliding my penis inside Elder Grant. An asshole could become a sex organ if it interacted with a penis. Just like a mouth. As long as I didn't touch Elder Grant's penis, though, his asshole would remain just an asshole.

Elder Grant's body convulsed, his asshole clenched, and I knew he'd come. Before he could do anything else, I whirled him around, grabbing his cupped hand. I pulled it toward my face in the dark and licked his palm clean. I almost gagged, having never even managed before to swallow my own semen, but I got every last drop off his hand. Then I stood up.

"It-it's not sex if you swallow my load?" Elder Grant whispered with a note of despair.

"Not if I don't get it straight from your dick." If he could use sex words, I could, too. That still didn't make it either oral or anal intercourse. The fact that what we'd done didn't fit into either category proved it wasn't sex.

He pulled me against him, and we hugged tightly for almost a minute. Then he whispered in my ear. "What about you?"

"I'll just jack off like usual."

"Really? You don't want me—"

"Turn around."

I dropped to my knees again and resumed licking my companion's asshole while I beat off into my hand. It didn't take long. I stood up and turned Elder Grant back toward me again.

"I don't think I can…" he began.

"Let's just smell my cum together," I whispered. I raised my hand, and I could feel my companion's breath in the darkness. I wasn't able to face eating my own load after ejaculating, but I felt something more was needed to cap the experience.

"Turn around," I said.

"Again?"

I positioned him facing his cot once more and again pried open his back slit. This time, though, I wiped my palm covered in cum up and down his crack.

He gasped.

I closed his flaps, pulled him close, and kissed the back of his neck. "Buona notte, caro," I whispered.

"S-sogni d'oro," he whispered back.

The color of my dreams, though, was slightly darker than sandy but lighter than brown.

***

After I reached over to turn off my alarm the next morning, I lay in the dark for another few minutes until Elder Grant pulled up the serranda and let the early morning light in. I was afraid to look at him. What if he was sorry about last night? What if he felt compelled to repent and call the mission president? We'd only masturbated, but I knew President Kimball in Salt Lake was disgusted by gays. I'd read *Il Miracolo del Perdono* in English before my mission and in Italian again here. Elder Packer in the Quorum of the Twelve downright loathed us. Even if Elder

Grant and I hadn't done anything *really* bad, I understood that life as I knew it could be over by the end of the day.

"Buona mattina," I ventured, grateful my voice didn't crack.

Spaccavoce.

Elder Grant walked over to my cot and leaned down. "Ciao, caro," he whispered before giving me a peck on the lips. Morning breath was incredible, I realized. It meant someone loved me enough to get close even at his worst.

How could life ever get any better than it was right now?

If only Heavenly Father could kill me before I loused everything up.

"Another day full of opportunity to serve the Lord."

I sat on the edge of my cot and watched as my companion headed to the bathroom. I brushed a couple of ants off my arm and thanked Heavenly Father for the wonderful day ahead.

Chapter Two:
David Hedison's Referral

Mornings after we left the apartment at 9:30 were dedicated to 24-hour work. Even being rebuffed by man after man with no interest in our message couldn't bring me down today. What was difficult was not dragging Elder Grant into an alley to make out with him. I wondered if it would be okay to return to Lovers' Lane some evening and beat off together while we watched all those cars with newspapers taped over their windows rocking back and forth.

I'd been infatuated with Elder Grant from the first day I arrived in Napoli. Most missionaries arriving in an area had to find their new apartment on their own, hard enough even if we weren't carrying everything we owned in two huge suitcases. But Elder Grant had been waiting for me— alone—at the station. It wasn't long before I noticed other qualities: every time he emptied the trash can beside his desk, he'd empty mine as well; and our very first P-Day a week after we met, he spent the day writing out the most important verses from the Book of Mormon in large print for an elderly member with poor eyesight.

We wandered around Piazza Plebiscito this morning, past the shops in the glass-covered Galleria, and even into the old castle along the waterfront which was used these days as Napoli's City Hall.

"Non mi interesse."

"Scusate."

"Ho fretta."

The translation was always the same: "Get lost."

Being torn down like this virtually every moment we were out of the apartment left most of us so fragile I wondered if other companionships found unorthodox ways to cope with the stress. I knew Elder Bennett liked going to the roughest neighborhoods in Cagliari to provoke hoodlums he could then try to beat up. Elder Swanson had been caught twice with straight porn in his suitcase after traveling alone during transfers.

I almost *wanted* an unpleasant confrontation with a stranger on the street so Elder Grant and I would have more stress to relieve later.

But as the hours passed without any exceptionally rude interactions, all I could think about was getting my companion behind closed doors again. I selected a few postcards I hoped would always remind me of this incredible day, the day after yesterday evening's incredible night, in this incredible place. The Mergellina lit up at dusk, Castel Sant'Elmo protecting the city, and the funicolare creeping its way uphill.

We'd sung "Funicolí, funicolá!" in Culture Capsule every Sunday night in the Missionary Training Center.

"Buon giorno," Elder Grant said, stopping a gentleman in a tailored wool business suit that clearly cost more than our off-the-rack polyester ones. The man looked a bit like David Hedison from *Voyage to the Bottom of the Sea*. "Siamo rappresentanti della Chiesa de Gesú Cristo—"

How could I have a crush on Captain Crane when I was only six years old? Two years before the age of accountability?

The man held up a hand and started to walk past. I gave a little shrug to encourage Elder Grant not to take the rejection to heart. Elder Young in Cagliari had had a nervous breakdown over his feelings of rejection, sitting down in the middle of the street crying, and had quickly been sent back to Boise. It was technically an "honorable release," but we all knew the cool reception he'd receive in his home ward.

A moment later, David Hedison turned back toward us.

"Look," he said, "I'm not interested. I don't believe in God." He shook his head rather smugly. "But my sister might want to talk to you. She's a devout Catholic, but she's been very depressed lately, and if you can cheer her up a little, maybe what you're doing isn't entirely useless."

Just *mostly* useless, I realized he was saying. It was still nicer than a lot of comments we heard.

"Her name's Elisabetta," the man continued, jotting down an address. "I'm afraid she's in the Quartieri Spagnoli."

At least it wasn't the Rione Sanitá.

"Do you think she's home now?" Elder Grant asked.

"Unless she's out buying some tomatoes. It's good to try her during the day, though. That neighborhood's not very nice at night."

"Thanks, Signor...?"

The man started to walk off again but hesitated one last time. "She likes aranciata."

We watched him continue whatever errand he'd been on for another few moments until he was lost in the crowd. "Good job," I said. "He could see the Spirit in your eyes."

"Thank you, Anziano Mortensen, but if he was responding to the joy in my countenance, it's because you put it there."

Words like that weren't sappy when the person you loved said them about *you*. "I saw a picture of you in E.U.R. from one of the other elders before we ever met," I said. "And you already had a beautiful countenance."

"Aw, shucks." Elder Grant laughed. "Flattery will get you a handful of cum."

"Ottimo," I returned. "Your shoes are polished nicely, too. And that tie is really sharp. And you ironed your shirt quite well. And—"

"Per caritá! How much cum do you think I have?"

I tried to think of a clever reply but couldn't. "Well," I said, "you do have limited storage capacity, so we'll have to keep emptying you out to give you a chance to refill." If only I could tell him I had plenty of room in my rectum. But that would be sex, and we couldn't do anything that sinful.

"If we pop into a bar to get an aranciata for Elisabetta, we can use their bathroom." Elder Grant paused. "Do you have someplace to put what I've got stored up right now?"

I licked my lips. "I'll think of something."

***

Elisabetta lived only a few streets over from Spaccanapoli, the long, straight thoroughfare that had sliced directly through old Napoli for centuries. From the right vantage point up on the hill, one could look down and understand immediately why the street had acquired its nickname.

Some areas along the infamous street were reasonably nice, while others, like the part nearest Elisabetta's apartment, were subtly depressing. Subtly only because one grew accustomed so quickly to the garbage and filth everywhere. Relatives who came to visit my family in New Orleans often commented on how much trash lay on the streets of the French Quarter. But the garbage level of Napoli was three orders of magnitude more severe. Perhaps someone could come up with a Mercalli scale for filth and decay.

I didn't want to imagine what the city must have looked like back in 1656 when over 150,000 people, almost 60% of its residents, had died of the plague.

When I'd sent some photos of the present-day Forcella neighborhood home to my parents, Mom had commented that Napoli seemed rather quaint.

"No, Mom," I'd written back, "it's not quaint. It's only quaint if the image is four by six inches in front of you. When it's *everywhere*, it's brutal." Yet these days, only a few weeks later, I hardly thought about it anymore, only if something struck me as unnaturally dirtier than usual. Like the elderly woman in front of us who slipped on some dog feces and then sat down hard on the rest of the mess not clinging to her shoe.

"Merde!" she shouted.

True enough.

Elder Grant and I hurried to help her up, and she instinctively reached back to rub her sore behind, pulling away her hand in disgust.

My companion retreated a step. Fortunately, I carried a cloth handkerchief with me at all times, something my trainer in Quartu had taught me. It was an easy way to appear helpful when you really hadn't done anything all that difficult.

Elder Grant picked up the woman's bag of groceries— three rosette and a couple of etti of salami. He tried to be nonchalant while inspecting the bag for evidence of contamination, but the old woman could see his searching gaze and grabbed the bag from him. "Grazie," she muttered, not sounding at all grateful, but then there was no reason she should be. Who wouldn't be angry in her situation?

"Possiamo accompagnarle a casa?" I asked.

Her eyes flitted from my nametag to Elder Grant's. "No."

And who could blame her for feeling suspicious as well? A cousin of mine doing his mission in Illinois told me the missionaries there tried to recruit teens to play basketball but then used that to pressure them to come to church. An RM in my ward told me that on his mission to Japan, they "taught English," but the words they taught were things like "church," "gospel," "atonement," and "tithing." In Quartu, Elder Cornett and I did a weekly radio show. We'd play pop songs like Barbra Streisand's "Woman in Love" or ELO's "All over the World." In between songs, we'd read a few minutes from our missionary discussions.

No listeners ever called the station and asked us to come teach them the rest.

The old woman tossed the soiled handkerchief onto the street and walked away. A young boy, maybe five, threw down the cigarette butt he'd just picked up and grabbed the handkerchief instead, running off with his find.

Sometimes, it was easier to handle the things I witnessed by pretending I was Will Robinson in an episode of *Lost in Space*, exploring life on a newly discovered planet.

I wondered if the director had meant for Dr. Smith to seem so gay?

While I identified with Nellie Oleson's brother in *Land of the Giants*, I felt nothing for his bank robber friend. It was Don Marshall I couldn't keep my eyes off of. But I told my parents I watched the series every week because one of the flight attendants was Mormon.

We knocked on Elisabetta's door a few minutes later. She lived two flights up in a building with yellow paint fading to gray in places. The stairwell showed what appeared to be unhealthy cracks, but as inspectors hadn't insisted on adding beams to support it, I assumed the damage was only superficial. Against the outer wall of each landing, someone had set up a memorial for a deceased loved one. Almost all of the photos were of young men.

"Chi é?" asked the woman who answered the door. She wore a plain black dress. Women in southern Italy often wore black after the death of their husband or a parent. Mormons in America might wear black to a funeral and keep their mourning clothes stored away until needed again. I knew a Jewish family that had mourning rituals, something to do with a mirror, if I remembered correctly, that lasted a whole week, with some other kind of commemoration at the end of a year. But southern Italian women often wore black *every day for the rest of their lives*, even if they started at the age of thirty. They'd discard all of their previous clothing and only buy black from that point on. Times were changing, but they would never change for some people, and I sensed Elisabetta was one of them.

"Buon giorno," Elder Grant said. "Il suo fratello ci ha chiesto di visitarle."

"Davvero?"

"He said you were having a bit of a hard time and might like someone to talk to."

At that, the woman laughed. "Talk?" She chuckled again, but it quickly turned into a sigh. "Sure. Why not? Come on in."

Elders were never supposed to be alone with women. Sister missionaries were never supposed to be alone with men. But sometimes, we did what we had to do.

I handed Elisabetta the bottle of aranciata we'd purchased. Fanta. She took it with a smile, but she looked wary, not pleased.

Her apartment was simply furnished, though everything appeared to be in good condition, and the place looked spotless. On one wall was a framed print of Mary holding baby Jesus. To the left, several inches lower, was a photo of a man about Elisabetta's age, taken in a portrait studio. To the right, at the same height as the photo of the forty-year-old man, was a photo of a twenty-year-old man, also taken professionally.

I recognized the young man from the memorial out on the stairwell landing.

On a tiny table underneath the portrait of Mary sat a simple ceramic vase, blue, that held three fresh daisies—happy, cheerful flowers. Maybe her brother was wrong about her. Perhaps she was already recovering from her loss.

Elder Grant and I sat on the sofa. Before she would take a chair near us, Elisabetta asked if she could offer us anything. My companion deferred, but I'd learned that being a slight imposition was more polite. "Un bicchiere d'acqua, per favore," I said, wanting her to keep the aranciata for herself. Elisabetta disappeared into the kitchen and returned shortly with a glass.

Mineral water, I recognized from the bubbles. I loved the stuff, but I'd hoped for tap, since mineral water could be expensive. I usually only splurged on it once or twice a month myself. I smiled and took a sip.

Porca vacca. It was Acqua Ferrarelle, probably the most expensive mineral water out there, with an unmistakable flavor. Elisabetta had just served me the equivalent of champagne, something clearly reserved for special guests.

I felt like a heel.

"Signora…?" I began.

"Coticelli," she said.

"Signora Coticelli, quest'acqua é proprio incredibile." I figured it best to pretend it was my first time, making her sacrifice more meaningful.

"Le piace?" She smiled.

"Mi da le palpitazioni." It was a bit over the top, but the David Hedison lookalike had asked us to make his sister feel better, and that was always the right thing to do, whether she was depressed or not, whether or not she was interested in the Church.

"You speak Italian so well."

Elder Grant rolled his eyes at my undeserved praise. It wasn't hard to sound educated. Almost any word in English ending with -tion was essentially the same in Italian, only with a -zione at the end instead. Inclinazione, maturazione, perturbazione, and, of course, masturbazione. I could use a "big word" in Italian I'd never seen or heard even once just by making an educated guess.

I sometimes used "big words" in English, too, without meaning to sound snooty. I'd mentioned something in Elders' Quorum once about carcinogens in New Orleans drinking water.

"Ooh, carcinogens," the first councilor said in a mocking tone.

I'd had no idea that was a pretentious word. I just tried to use words appropriate to the topic at hand. I'd been using the impurity of New Orleans tap water as a metaphor.

"Ooh, metaphor," the first councilor mocked when I explained.

"Thank you, Signora," I said. "But we'd really like to hear what *you* have to say. Your brother said life's been difficult lately."

Elisabetta sighed again, but not as heavily as before. "It's not just lately," she said. "Ernesto cheated on me all the time. He…brought things home." She closed her eyes for a moment. "It was a relief when he left."

I saw her eying my glass of mineral water and wished I had something useful to offer her.

"Your husband left you?" Elder Grant repeated.

"He didn't come home one evening." She shrugged. "I never heard from him again. He either ran off or got killed by some other woman's husband. But I never heard from the police, so who knows?"

I was amazed sometimes at the things perfect strangers would tell us. While we were out tracting one day, a woman had confided, standing right in her doorway, not even inside with her door closed, that she'd had an affair with the portiere in her building. A man told us he'd stolen money from his brother-in-law and asked us for advice on how to resolve the rift in his family. An elderly woman asked if we thought she should tell her middle child, in his fifties, he had a different father from his siblings.

"Not knowing what happened must have been difficult," I said, looking from Elisabetta to the photo of her husband. He reminded me of Michael York's best friend in *Logan's Run*. I'd been shocked by a sex scene in the novel I'd purchased after seeing the movie. Logan was forced to have sex five times in a row and was in agony by the end.

"It was hard on Enea," she said. "He was only eleven."

Signora Coticelli went on to talk about her son's truancy, then his shoplifting, then his introduction to housebreaking, low level drug dealing, and finally doing things for the Camorra he could no longer tell his mother about.

"He wasn't a bad boy," she said. "He just knew I needed the money. And I *did* need it. So what could I do?" She looked at the photo on the wall. "I let him do those terrible things. And it killed him." She absentmindedly fiddled with a crucifix hanging from a thin necklace. "If it was wrong for Ernesto to cheat on me, what I did to my son was a hundred times worse." She sighed. "A thousand times."

Elder Grant and I exchanged glances. I could see him mouthing a suggestion we give her a blessing, but I shook my head. We needed to do something that could provide a more tangible benefit.

"My brother is worried I'm unhappy." Elisabetta laughed again but without mirth. "I deserve to be unhappy."

"Signora Coticelli," Elder Grant said softly, "the gospel of Jesus Christ can bring peace and forgiveness to everyone."

I could feel my companion shift into missionary mode. Every week, we had to turn in our stats to our zone leaders, who then sent them to the mission president in Rome. In addition to the number of hours worked—sixty; lessons taught—seven; hours spent in individual and companion study—twelve and six, respectively; we had several other hard and fast quotas not to be missed under any circumstances: get addresses from fifteen random people we stopped on the street, bring at least one person to church, have at least one person committed to baptism, and baptize at least one person. The next week, we had to bring yet another new person to church, the person who had come to church the previous week we now needed firmly committed to baptism, and the person committed to baptism the week before now had to physically be baptized. We were ordered to keep that pipeline flowing without any clogs.

Of course, that pipeline was filled with nothing *but* clogs. Clogs that could only be cleared, we were told at every zone conference, if we demonstrated more faith.

I held up a hand and said, in English, without taking my eyes away from Elisabetta's pained face, "We're going to help her in whatever way works best for *her*."

"But having the gospel—"

"Is more painful for some people than not having it."

I often daydreamed about what it must be like to be gay without knowing it was wrong. The Church taught that we were only responsible to live up to the amount of truth we had. Sometimes, I wondered if sending missionaries out into the world wasn't the absolute worst thing the Church could do for humanity.

Signora Coticelli frowned, probably suspecting we were saying something bad about her. One of the mission rules was that if we ever did need to speak English, we weren't to do it in front of Italians.

"Signora," I said, "is there something you do that brings you even a few minutes of happiness?" I wasn't sure what to say, what to ask, but I wanted to talk about something, anything, that wasn't the Church.

"Happiness?" She shook her head. "My brother sends me postcards from the cities he travels to for work. I like looking at all the different places he's been."

I wanted to ask if she had a photo album she could show us, but I was afraid she might never have been able to afford one, and the request would be insensitive. What if I asked if she had a box of photos and postcards, and she felt insulted I didn't expect her to have an album?

What if sharing her photos was simply too personal an act?

"Sometimes," she said, "I listen to the radio. Or I walk past the flower stalls. Or I go up to Vomero and look down on the city. It's so pretty…from a distance."

I laughed, causing both Elisabetta and my companion to frown. "Can I quote you on that?"

"Non capisco."

"I was just saying something similar to my mother."

Signora Coticelli smiled sadly. "Are you close to your mother?"

And suddenly, I knew what to give Elisabetta. "Yes, it's hard being away for two years. We can't even call."

"You can't phone her on her birthday? On Christmas?" Her eyes narrowed as she glanced at our scriptures and flip charts.

"We write once a week."

Elisabetta's shoulders relaxed a little. "You write your mother?" she asked. "Every week?"

"Every week."

She turned to look at the photos on her wall.

"What was Enea's favorite meal?" I asked.

"Anziano…"

Signora Coticelli frowned again. She studied our faces for several more seconds. "He liked lasagna."

I smiled. Of course he did. So expensive and time-consuming to make it was often the special holiday meal for Christmas. "Signora Coticelli," I said, "how do you feel about us dropping off all the cheeses and meats and everything else you'll need? We can bring it by Thursday morning and then stop by for dinner later so you can tell us some stories about Enea."

Elisabetta's smile looked genuine. I could tell by the crinkles next to her eyes. Polite smiles didn't make crinkles.

Chapter Three:
You're Still the One

Elder Grant and I were back on Via Nicolardi by 9:07, too soon to go back inside the apartment. If the zone leaders were in, they'd see we'd stopped working before 9:30. *They* could be in the apartment any time of the day or evening doing "leadership" tasks. The only work the rest of us were qualified to do was proselyting.

I pointed to a bar a block from our building. After purchasing a pack of candy made of pressed milk powder, we went back outside, where we let a couple of candies melt on our tongue. We had to keep a lookout for the other two companionships so that if they returned early, assuming they weren't already home, they wouldn't see we'd arrived in the neighborhood ahead of them.

"When I was being transferred back to the mainland from Sardinia," I said, suddenly aware there was finally someone I could tell my secrets to, "I was the only missionary on the ferry. I shared a tiny room with another man. He was in his thirties, looking kind of poor and a little rough. Not really my type. Smelled like smoke. I prefer guys like James Franciscus and John Cassavetes."

Elder Grant frowned.

"From *Longstreet* and *Rosemary's Baby*." There was something to be said for growing up away from mainstream Mormon culture. I didn't realize until my mission interviews that I wasn't supposed to watch R-rated movies. Hell, my mom even helped me sneak into *The Exorcist* by myself when I was still a deacon.

"Oh." Elder Grant didn't sound enlightened by my explanation. Or maybe he was simply unimpressed that neither man I'd mentioned looked like him.

"And guys like you."

"I always found older men attractive. Though I guess I've never been picky."

I decided to let that pass.

"But I figured he'd be rough enough that I could find a way to convince him to let me service him."

"Mannaggia. What did you say?"

I shrugged, opening another candy and chewing this one quickly rather than letting it melt. "I think I tried something like, 'These overnight ferry trips can be so stressful. What do you do to relieve the stress?'"

"And?"

"Turned out he didn't speak Italian. I think he might have been Rumeno."

"So what happened?"

"I thought about sleeping in the nude, maybe lying face down on my bunk before he went to sleep so that he could see me there, my ass ready to be taken advantage of. I kind of hoped he'd rape me. But I also wanted him to kill me when he was done so I wouldn't have to jump overboard to keep myself from confessing and being sent home."

Elder Grant put his hand on my shoulder.

"I couldn't do it, though, and not only because it was freezing. I'd have suffered through that. It was just that the idea of being the seducer made me feel…icky."

We stood for several more minutes in silence, not eating any more of the milk candies. Elder Grant never took his hand off my shoulder.

***

My companion's dick was a little over seven inches long. It had a slight curve, with a medium girth at the bottom, tapering slightly near the top, with a large head. His cock didn't quite look like a mushroom, but it was close. I'd heard classmates of mine at the University of New Orleans talking once about psychedelic mushrooms, but eating such things couldn't possibly create a greater sense of wellbeing and awe than the spores that came out of Elder Grant.

My own penis was much shorter, probably only five and a half inches, but it was as big around as a fifty-cent piece. Maybe even a bit more, but not as fat as an Eisenhower dollar. Mine was also darker than Elder Grant's, darker than the skin on the rest of my body. The head didn't have as much overhang as my companion's, but given my girth, it was still larger overall than Elder Grant's.

I wanted to touch his penis, and Elder Grant's fingers came awfully close to mine, but we knew we couldn't make contact, so he demonstrated his as if showing off a car or boat on a game show, and I moved mine about in different positions as if demonstrating how a flexible desk lamp worked.

"Are you sorry mine isn't as long as yours?" I asked.

"Are you sorry mine isn't as wide as yours?" he returned.

"I've always rather liked my dick, and I like yours, too."

"Your nipples aren't quite like mine, either," Elder Grant noted. "Pointier, with a harder base. And your ass is different. Your hole is a little lower than mine."

"At least I can touch all your other parts."

Elder Grant folded his blanket on the floor. "Lie on top of me," he said. We'd already determined that the cot squeaked too loudly to risk, whether we tried anything while the others were out of the apartment or not. If they returned before we finished, there'd be no way to get off the cot without making suspicious noises.

Elder Grant lay face down on the floor. I kneeled beside him, threw a leg across his body like I was getting on a horse, leaned forward, and eased myself down onto him as if he were a mattress.

"Stop supporting yourself with your elbows," he said. "I want to feel *all* of your weight on me."

I relaxed and felt myself sink down into him.

"Ahhh," we both said at the same time.

But I could feel my dick stiffening against his ass. That would count as Elder Grant directly stimulating my sex organ. I put my weight back on my arms and slowly pulled myself off of him. "Turn over," I said, and he did as I asked. "Spread your legs." The stone floor was cold even in the summer, so I put my own blanket down as well. Then I lay below him, my face just reaching his crotch. "Jack off while I lick your balls."

We'd spent half an hour during Dual Study learning a few more words that would make our intimate conversations easier.

While licking Elder Grant's testicles, my nose accidentally brushed against his hand as he moved it up and down his shaft. I hadn't touched his dick itself, but I could tell ball-licking was going to be too dangerous to include as a regular part of our masturbation sessions. I scooted a few inches down and just watched, the difference like viewing *Alien* from the first or second row instead of from the rear of the theater.

I gasped in synchronization with Elder Grant when something spurted out of him. It landed on his stomach, most falling directly into his navel.

I scooted forward again, my sternum on top of my companion's dick. It wouldn't matter now that he was no longer susceptible to stimulation. I licked the cum off his stomach, dug my tongue into his navel, and sucked as much of the rest out as I could. The taste was still not quite pleasant but irresistible all the same.

"Now I want you to stand," Elder Grant said. "With one foot on either side of me. I'll lie here and watch you beat off over me."

I stood and started stroking myself while looking down at him. It was hard not to get on my knees and rub one hand across his chest while my other tried to bring me closer to climax. I wanted to touch his face, put my fingers in his mouth, grab his sack. Instead, I grabbed mine and squeezed slightly while I stroked myself faster and faster. My eyes closed automatically when I felt myself getting close, but I forced them open so I could watch Elder Grant's face.

"Ohh unnhhh!" I groaned. I'd planned to let my cum land wherever it might, hopefully on my companion's face so I could lick it off, but at the last second, I caught it with my hand. One drop landed on his neck, though, and another high on his right cheek just below his eye.

Elder Grant made no sound, but he smiled as if he'd just seen a sunrise. He rubbed a finger across his cheek and licked it.

I stepped to the side.

"Put the rest on your asshole," he commanded. "You got to lick mine last night. It's my turn now."

I wiped as much of my cum onto my asshole as I could, feeling a little guilty. *Before* I came last night, I couldn't get enough of either Elder Grant's ass or his cum. But *after* cumming tonight, I felt that expecting my companion to lick cum off my asshole was asking too much, especially since *he'd* already cum, too.

When Elder Grant got up on his knees, though, and dug his face into my backside, he seemed to genuinely enjoy himself. After ten or fifteen seconds, I couldn't even worry about it any longer, luxuriating in both the new physical sensation and the accompanying understanding of the love that came along with it.

***

Things were always a little hectic on the one day each week the sisters came to our apartment. The one exception for elders and sisters not to be alone with the opposite sex was the weekly district meeting, but even then, we had to keep the front door open so that other residents of the building passing by our apartment and hearing laughter would have no reason to suspect impropriety.

At least one district in each zone usually included sister missionaries. For us, it was Napoli 2. While every district in the mission had either four or six elders, no district ever included more than four sisters in one apartment.

"They spend too much time in the bathroom," President Alsop joked during the last zone conference. Almost every missionary had laughed, it seemed, but I'd noticed Sorella Bruzzone wasn't one of them.

She was still junior, to Sorella Franklin. Our other two sisters were Burns, from Wyoming, and Kembleford, from Australia. Sorella Kembleford could have been a model. Sister Burns already had a degree in Childhood Education. Sorella Bruzzone, from Genova, reminded me of a woman scientist from 1950's sci-fi movies, pretty but made up deliberately not to appear too attractive so that her colleagues would pay more attention to what she said than how she looked. Sister Franklin, from Utah, was threatening neither physically nor intellectually. She asked, "Have you found a family to baptize today?" almost every time we saw each other, even if it was Preparation Day or Sunday at church.

From my bedroom, I could hear that Sorelle Bruzzone and Franklin had arrived. "We better get out there, Anziano," I said. I grabbed a bundle of clothes and ducked into the bathroom to throw them in the washing machine, the first time we'd agreed to wash our clothes together. I lingered just a moment over a pair of his garments. Because they were cotton, they showed the cum I'd shot on them last night, and yesterday morning, and the previous night. It was risky to wear the same pair of garments that long in the summer heat, but Elder Grant said he enjoyed wearing my cum too much. I assured him I could fully cum another pair, and he finally let me take them. I gave them a last sniff now. I expected any reliable olfactometer would have registered some alarming numbers, but I just smiled and then joined the zone leaders and the other two elders in our tiny kitchen, where the two sisters were sitting. We only had six chairs, no two of which matched, so only the sisters and ZLs would be able to sit for the meeting.

"The other sisters didn't come with you?" asked Elder Murdock.

"They're on Mormon Standard Time." Sister Franklin laughed.

Sorella Bruzzone rolled her eyes. She understood English well enough, but she rarely spoke it. The White Bible, a slim, vinyl-covered volume of mission rules we carried at all times, demanded that even inside the apartment, whether Italians were present or not, we never lapse into English. If no Italian missionaries were in the district, elders were often accused of "trying to be bravo" if they stuck to Italian in private.

"Why don't I sing a solo while we wait?" Sister Franklin suggested in English.

I'd softly sung "You're Still the One" last night in the dark until Elder Grant fell asleep.

"Dio mio," Sorella Bruzzone huffed. "Sono stanchissimo di 'America the Beautiful.'"

"Hymns are uplifting," Sister Franklin said.

"'America the Beautiful' non é un inno," Sorella Bruzzone countered.

And it wasn't in Italian, I noted, though I felt it best not to get involved.

"America is the only nation free enough for the gospel to be restored." Sister Franklin stood next to her chair and cleared her throat. She reminded me somehow of Florence Foster Jenkins, though Sister Franklin had a better voice. I remembered reruns of old radio shows like *The Shadow* that played on a station I listened to when I was a kid. I even bought an album of Orson Welles's 1938 *War of the Worlds* broadcast. The old silent movies that aired every Friday night on Channel 12 were fun, too. Lon Chaney in *The Hunchback of Notre Dame* and *Phantom of the Opera*.

And now I was reminded of *Phantom of the Paradise*.

I always felt a little guilty for lusting after Paul Williams, and not only because he was a man.

"La la la la la," Sister Franklin cooed. The district leader in Quartu used to sing in the shower. The rest of us used to go out on the balcony, even in bad weather, until he was done.

"Laaaa!"

What was taking Elder Grant so long, I wondered. He was missing everything. While it probably reflected poorly on our character, it was fun to analyze the other missionaries and how well they got along. Any conversation on the topic always left us feeling luckier than ever to be together.

"Siamo fortunati," I'd say.

"Beati," Elder Grant would reply.

"You Americans," Sorella Bruzzone said, "think you're the only people in the world with any freedom."

Anziani Crandall and Hatch, the other two elders from our apartment, joined us in the kitchen, pushing past the rest of us and standing near the doors leading to the balcony.

"Have you found a family to baptize today?" Sister Franklin asked them.

"Uh, we haven't even been outside yet."

"Then you probably should have found someone yesterday."

"Anziano Grant!" I called down the hallway.

"Italians aren't free," Sister Franklin said, turning back to her companion. "What isn't ruled by the Catholic Church is controlled by the Camorra or the Mafia or the Communists."

Sorella Bruzzone shrugged. "I was free to stay Catholic. I was free to convert to Mormonism and serve as a missionary. I'm free to stop being Mormon any time I want. I could go home right now. Do *you* have that freedom?"

"The freedom to sin?" Sister Franklin turned up her nose. "Pfft! It's just like an Italian to talk about quitting."

"Anziano Grant!" I called again.

The other elders watched the exchange in silence, as if observing a Road Show in their stake center back home.

"So you could leave the religion of your family like I did if you wanted to?"

"That's got nothing to do with being an American," Sister Franklin said through tight lips. "Our only lack of freedom comes from God." She clapped her hand over her mouth when she realized what she'd said.

Sorella Bruzzone leaned back and smiled, turning to the zone leaders. "She can't sing with her mouth covered."

Elder Murdock turned to me wearily. "Go get your companion so we can start."

I hurried down the hall and found Elder Grant straightening his tie. I waved for him to follow, and he thrust a "clean" pair of my garments toward me, showing a splatter of fresh cum. When I grabbed onto them, he wouldn't let go, and we both pulled in a brief tug-of-war. I thought about the spaghetti scene from *Lady and the Tramp*. I held the underwear to my face, breathing in deeply.

Elder Grant put his nose next to mine. We both held the cummy garments to our faces, inhaled like the woman next door did on her balcony when she went out for a morning smoke in the fresh air, and then laughed.

I wondered if I'd ever be able to put on clean garments again, if they were all going to be pre-loaded from now on.

"Anziani!"

I thrust the garments under my pillow, wishing I could throw Elder Grant onto the cot instead. I touched my companion's fingers for a moment, and then we joined the others in the kitchen just as the final two sisters walked in the door.

Sister Franklin started the meeting with her rendition of "America the Beautiful."

Sorella Bruzzone filed her nails.

Chapter Four:
Be Prepared

We stopped in front of a Madonna box covered with glass so dirty we could barely see the statue inside. An old woman glanced up and kissed her crucifix as she paused before walking on. "Do you ever feel like two different people?" I asked my companion. I remembered an English professor in my first survey course saying women were often depicted in literature as either Madonnas or whores.

"Like being a missionary and a regular person at the same time?"

"Not exactly." It was deeper than that. I'd been reflecting on it a lot lately, but I still wasn't sure it was possible to clearly express my confusion.

"Being American versus being Mormon?" Elder Grant guessed again. "Speaking both English and Italian?"

Two Vespas whizzed past us in quick succession.

"I was thinking more of being both Dr. Jekyll and Mr. Hyde." I'd seen the 1931 version starring Fredric March first, but even the 1920 silent movie was worth viewing more than once.

"Per caritá!"

"One minute, an elderly Relief Society member at church is writing a poem about how kind I am. The next, I'm about to curse out the seven-year-old on the bus who keeps stepping on my foot."

Elder Grant's concern turned into laughter.

But I changed direction again. "One minute, I'm proud of myself for putting cement in two empty detergent boxes my first week in every district and making a barbell." While I'd always hated team sports, I'd discovered in junior high that exercise in general could be fun. I liked jogging, too, and I hoped to try running a half-marathon one day.

"I love watching you work out."

"And the next minute," I continued, "I'm fantasizing about doing naked push-ups with you lying face down underneath me, holding your cheeks apart."

Our eyes met for a moment, and then Elder Grant looked off toward Vesuvius. He stared for a long time, and I was afraid to interrupt him. Finally, he turned back to me, leaning forward slightly. "You know," he almost whispered, "I only found out for the first time I had an Uncle Stuart when he sent me a present for my high school graduation." He shook his head. "Springsteen's *Born to Run*. Boy, was my dad upset." He stared in the direction of Vesuvius again.

I followed Elder Grant's gaze, as if the volcano might somehow provide a clue or a hint or, *magari*, a direct answer to help solve our predicament. But Vesuvius wasn't a god, even if it was named after the son of Zeus. "Was your uncle…?"

"I hope masturbating together gets this gay stuff out of our system."

Another woman stopped in front of the Madonna box, set her two jugs of wine on the pavement, and said a brief prayer before picking them up again and moving on. "Kids drink wine here by the time they're ten," I said, "but I think there's less alcoholism in Italy than in the States."

Elder Grant's brows furrowed. "I may not be addicted to panettone," he pointed out, "but I sure intend to eat one every Christmas from now on." He looked down at the black stones of the street. "If I can find them when I get back to America." He turned to me as if searching for the answer Vesuvius hadn't given him. "I don't want to end up the funny uncle no one talks about."

Now it was my turn to frown. "When will you tell your family about me?" I asked.

Elder Grant's brows furrowed more deeply.

"So I'm already a funny uncle." Our eyes locked again. When I smiled, my companion didn't laugh. But then, it wasn't a very funny thing for a funny uncle to say.

***

On our way home after spending another evening with Sister Coticelli, I pulled Elder Grant to the side. "Che c'é?" he asked.

I removed my thick name tag from my shirt pocket and shoved it in my pants. Then I handed Elder Grant my scriptures.

"Non capisco."

"Anziano," I said, "I'm stepping into this drugstore to pick up some condoms."

My companion's eyes grew wide. "But…but…"

"Weren't you an Eagle scout?" I asked. The Church left us little choice about participating. Always hoping no one would guess my secret, I'd been disappointed to discover it was possible to be good at pull-ups and still not be seen as a "real man" by other guys. But with merit badges for numismatics and philatelics, I wasn't the manliest of the boys in my troop.

"The motto was never 'Be Prepared to Sin.'"

"We won't be sinning."

"Anziano…"

"Torno subito."

I entered the drugstore and looked about, hoping that as a single man, no one would realize I was a missionary, despite the white shirt. The aisles were narrow, though, and I was afraid the longer I was there, the greater my risk of discovery. Best just to ask for what I needed.

"Avete i preservativi?" I tried to sound casual.

"How many?" the young woman asked without interest.

I really had no idea and just guessed. "Ten?" That didn't sound definitive enough. And I didn't want to have to come back any sooner than necessary. "I mean, twenty."

At this, the young woman smiled but fortunately offered no comment.

Any expense beyond the essential was devastating to our budget. We were supposed to live on $250 a month. Even with the favorable exchange rate, I often cashed an extra check for $20 before the end of the month so I didn't have to live a completely Spartan life, enjoying a Margherita pizza here, a calzone there. I'd saved up over $1200 before my mission helping one of the members of the ward install attic insulation, but that money was long gone. My dad wasn't poor, but I knew paying for my mission was still a challenge for him.

"And how about an enema bulb?" I asked. "Two." God only knew if "clistere" was the correct word. Sometimes, smaller dictionaries didn't have all the words I wanted to know, but the larger dictionaries had so many it was difficult to grasp the nuances. I'd spent my first several months in Italy talking about catching the "Pullman." My trainer had told me that was the word for "bus." I knew Pullman was the name of certain railway cars and figured the same guy might have designed a bus. So I kept saying "Pullman." Until Elder Grant told me on our first day together that "Pullman" referred to the fancy coaches that drove long distances from city to city. A local bus was just called an "autobus."

It seemed too easy.

The young woman helped me find what I needed. I handed over some lire, grabbed my bag, and joined my companion back on the sidewalk.

"Can we go now?" he asked as I slipped my nametag back on.

"Sure, Anziano. We just need to make one more stop first."

"Biscotti?" he asked hopefully.

"We need to buy a couple of zucchini." I rubbed my chin, trying to look contemplative, but I'd made the decision earlier. "We should start with relatively small ones, don't you think?"

Elder Grant's mouth fell open.

"No, no," I said. "We'll be putting them in a different hole."

***

One family near the Mergellina that let us teach them half a C had two large Capodimonte porcelain figurines on a bureau underneath a huge mirror with a gold frame at least six inches wide. One of the figurines depicted an elegant lady in ivory lace with a tiny dog. The other presented a group of six musicians wearing colorful upper class clothing from the late 18th century. The artwork was far too ornate and effete for my taste, reminding me of French aristocracy in the moments before they were carted off to the guillotine.

My scoutmaster had once called me effete. He wasn't the first councilor in the Elders' Quorum and so knew snooty words.

"Those were pretty figurines," Elder Grant said after we left the apartment and descended to the next floor.

"I can't believe you liked that!" I said, making an exaggerated grimace before slapping my forehead.

Elder Grant stuck his chin out in mock offense, thankfully not too deeply invested in his position. "What kind of art do *you* like?" he demanded.

A man in his thirties walking a greyhound passed us on his way up the stairs.

"Functional art, I guess, like mission-style lamps and mirrors and chairs." I'd been thinking about it throughout most of the lesson. Probably why the Spirit had departed and the family lost interest.

"Mission style?" Elder Grant asked suspiciously. "Our kitchen table is Early Junk Pile."

"Mission style is kind of related to the Craftsman style," I said, realizing I didn't have adequate words in either English or Italian. "A little like Arts and Crafts." I wasn't particularly knowledgeable about it myself. I only knew I liked the bold, strong lines of some of the pieces I'd seen.

"Boh."

"I wonder what kind of style I'd design if I had any talent myself?" I hated the Little Boy Blue painting my mother had hung in my childhood bedroom. She'd found an old lamp made of tiny Budweiser Clydesdales at a garage sale, though, and let me use that as a night light. I'd enjoyed the shiny horses well enough. My dad had bought me a horrible tie one Christmas featuring two men boxing. I could hardly imagine a more barbaric sport. The next year, he'd given me an even uglier tie with the New Orleans Jazz logo, a collector's item after the city sold the basketball team to Salt Lake. And then on my eighteenth birthday, he'd handed over a copy of *Be a Man! Males in Modern Society*. It was too academic for me to get through, almost certainly too academic for my father to have read more than the back cover blurb. He wasn't stupid, but he wasn't a reader, either. It was the title that was his message to me. "Nothing sporty," I said, "but I do like things that have a masculine feel."

"Plaid flannel shower curtains?" Elder Grant teased. "With a shower spout in the shape of a penis?"

I tapped my chin in faux concentration, feeling snooty for using the word "faux" even in my thoughts. "Do you think I can find something like that at J.C. Penney when I get home?" My companion smiled. "I don't want anything tacky," I clarified, "but maybe sheer curtains with male nude figures. Or how about light switch covers with military men, or male gymnasts, or bikers?" I wondered if I could find anything like that in the French Quarter.

"Geez, Elder."

"And for a coffee table, perhaps one of those steel toolboxes you see across the back of pickup trucks."

Elder Grant laughed again. "What would you put in your toolbox coffee table?"

I shrugged. "Probably my embroidery threads and hoops."

"Anziano, mi stai prendendo in giro."

"Can you believe they don't award merit badges for original embroidery design?"

I had a sudden flashback to Paul Lynde on *Hollywood Squares* answering the question, "Why do Hell's Angels wear leather?" with "Because chiffon wrinkles too easily."

For the first time, I realized he might be gay.

"Well, at least the toolbox part might work out if you can find a nice lesbian who wants to get married in the temple."

I didn't join him in his laughter, though. Instead, I took a deep breath, straightened my tie, and knocked on the next door.

***

We'd gotten through most of our first lesson with the family before the father looked confused at one of our questions and asked us one in return. "So you guys aren't Jehovah's Witnesses?" When we assured him we were not, he asked us to leave.

Two buildings later, a man on the third floor pulled back his head like a startled bird and suddenly spit in my face. I was too shocked to move, the man standing before me, smirking, with his hands on his hips. Before I could gather my senses, I felt Elder Grant take my arm and reposition me toward him. I felt him lick the spittle off my face slowly, gently caressing the back of my head as he did it.

Neither of us had ever been tempted to add spit to our jack off sessions, at least not for its own sake. My companion wasn't doing this to get a sexual thrill. He was doing it because he loved me. When he finished, we both turned to face the man at the door again. He was staring in horror.

"Buona sera," Elder Grant said before we walked off.

So when we returned to our apartment later, we both felt rather intensely the need for some physical love. For the past couple of weeks, we used our enema bulbs every evening to be prepared for whatever we might decide to do after Lights Out. Often, we used them again in the morning in case we felt inspired to be intimate again before we left the apartment for the day. Early morning intimacy, of course, required that we be especially quiet during Quiet Hour.

The easiest thing to do in the mornings, though, was pretty straightforward. Elder Grant liked to catch his cum when he ejaculated and wipe it across his freshly showered feet, on and in between his toes. Then I'd kneel before him and carefully lick every drop off. We figured if Jesus could wash his disciples' feet, we could lick off cum.

It was kind of our own Second Anointing.

Sometimes, we felt like doing something even simpler. Perhaps I'd shoot into the back of Elder Grant's garments, and he'd finish getting dressed without wiping it off or changing garments, wearing my cum the rest of the day. A couple of times, Elder Grant spread his cum all over my chest after I finished showering. I'd let it dry during Quiet Hour and then leave the apartment with dry cum under my white shirt and tie. Once, I shot into a condom, tied it off, and pushed it as far as I could up my companion's ass so that we could walk around all morning doing our 24-hour work knowing that if someone told him he was full of shit, he was really full of cum.

But the natural tendency to expel made that a one-time experiment. Thank goodness there was a little stone wall separating the campfire where the prostitutes worked at night in Vomero from the bus stop we needed.

We returned to shooting onto each other's ass. Or Elder Grant might wipe his cum onto my lips and then lick it off, perhaps have me pull down the top of my garments so he could wipe some cum on my nipples and lick that off before we left for the day. Something easy and quick.

We took more time in the evenings, preparing everything we needed before Lights Out. It might be another twenty or thirty minutes after the lights were extinguished, of course, before we finally retired for the night, though there were certainly times when we couldn't hold back and were finished in five minutes.

Tonight, Elder Grant carefully tore open a condom wrapper. I could hear him roll the rubber *preservativo* down over the zucchini he'd purchased that morning. He often used one shaped almost like his dick, minus the mushroomy head, while I used a cucumber on him that was shorter and fatter, closer matching my own.

Without any ability to see in the pitch-black bedroom, I could concentrate on my other senses. There seemed to be more than the traditional five. I didn't just mean the ESP of *The Sixth Sense*, though I did sometimes know what my companion craved without his needing to verbalize it in either English or Italian. And without a doubt, our proprioception seemed acutely attuned when we were intimate with each other, but it was more than that. My brain seemed to furnish an additional sense. I could "see" what we were doing as if the daytime sun were streaming through an uncovered window.

A zucchini wasn't sliding into my ass. That was Elder Grant's dick. I could see the veins. I could feel the increasing girth as he moved in deeper.

"Unh."

"Stai bene?"

"Sí."

It always hurt going in, no matter how many times we'd done this, no matter how gentle we tried to be. But the pain was replaced within seconds by pleasure.

I reached for a fresh condom to slide over the cucumber I had ready for my companion. Like a deaf Amy Irving learning to dance in *Voices* by concentrating on the vibrations in the floor, Elder Grant and I had learned to perform a carefully choreographed Tarantella of our own in the dark.

I applied hair conditioner to my condom-covered cucumber, a little more to Elder Grant's asshole, and we began fucking each other side by side, one hand pushing and pulling our proxy dicks while our other stroked the real ones.

"Ahh."

"Mmm."

We couldn't suppress the sounds completely but tried to muffle them as much as possible. We'd memorized by this point our average spurt distance and had bowls on Elder Grant's cot ready to catch our cum when we shot.

Wouldn't a *perfect* God have more than two arms? More than one cock, for that matter?

Maybe the paintings of God the Father were wrong. Perhaps Joseph Smith was keeping something from us we weren't ready to hear.

Elder Grant began pushing and pulling his proxy in and out of my ass more quickly, and I knew he was getting close. That sent a surge of testosterone through my system, and I could feel a deep tingling building inside my own dick as well.

I began fucking Elder Grant's ass faster and faster, keeping pace with the hand tugging on my real dick.

"Anziano…"

"Oh, Anziano…"

We rarely climaxed at the same time, didn't even try, but tonight, we both lurched violently in the darkness as we exploded at the same moment.

"Ahhh."

"Unhhh."

I felt a trickle of perspiration roll down my temple. Tomorrow, I vowed, while we were out working in the hot sun, I was going to lick off some of Elder Grant's sweat from his forehead.

My companion and I turned to each other in the dark, our lips drawn together by an invisible force, and slowly pulled our proxies out of each other as our tongues playfully continued our dance. We dropped the condom-covered vegetables onto the floor. I released my real dick and held my jack-off hand against Elder Grant's lips. He licked the cum off that hadn't fully escaped when I shot into the bowl. He offered me the back of his hand, which had a small but thick splotch of his own covering two knuckles.

But we still weren't finished. Like surgeons operating during a power outage, we blindly reached for the turkey basters we'd set beside our bowls before we started. I sucked up the pool of semen and seminal fluid in my bowl while Elder Grant sucked up the cum in his. I reached around and found my companion's asshole again, still lubricated enough to permit the filled baster past his sphincter. I slid it slowly in several inches.

I felt Elder Grant's baster tap against my lips and opened my mouth, letting the new proxy dick slide an inch along my tongue. With one hand holding my baster to his ass, I used my free hand to finger my asshole, pretending the conditioner on my fingertips was my companion's cum.

We didn't need to provide a signal, knowing instinctively to squeeze at the same instant. A short blast of Elder Grant's still warm cum hit the back of my throat.

My companion moaned softly as I withdrew my baster from his ass. After he pulled his proxy dick out of my mouth, we kissed again so I could give him the rest of his cum back. But then he passed it back to me yet again.

The gift that kept giving.

Chapter Five:

Feeling the Spirit

We were supposed to pick a single tracting zone and stick with it until we were finished. It was the only way to systematically approach a city this size. But neighborhoods like Ponticelli and Secondigliano could get awfully dreary. On the other hand, people in better areas felt little need to improve their lives, so tracting there was far less efficient. Elder Grant and I worked three tracting zones at the same time, flitting from one to the other on different days of the week. In addition, we threw in a session of "spirit tracting" every once in a while. And visits to our regular contacts always offered a little variety.

We worked the Mostra near the train station some mornings. The display boards were heavy and difficult to carry on the bus, but once they were set up, they freed us from hours of walking about trying to stop people on the street. Now we only had to approach anyone who dared try to read any of our display about the Book of Mormon, Joseph Smith, and the benefits of having a living prophet.

Most people seemed to have an innate understanding they had better not look.

On our way to visit Sister Coticelli one evening, we saw what were unmistakably small rivulets of blood between the black stones of the street only a block from her apartment. None of the other pedestrians seemed the least bit concerned.

Had someone clumsily dropped the cuts of beef they'd picked up from the butcher before they made it back home?

Elisabetta had told us on our last visit about the time one of Enea's toes had been cut off for some infraction he'd committed. Even then, she hadn't insisted he leave.

She'd banged her fist slowly against her cheek as she related the incident.

I planned to ask her about her grandparents when we visited today. And her favorite movies. And what kind of music she liked. And, of course, more about Enea.

"Anziani!" Sister Coticelli greeted us at her door with a smile. We always came prepared with both a bottle of aranciata and a bottle of Acqua Ferrarelle when we showed up. She brought both to the kitchen to open them while Elder Grant and I sat in the living room. After she returned with three glasses, she pulled out a small box of postcards.

The famed collection she'd hinted about for weeks. "Enea and I used to watch the fishermen coming back with their catch," she said, handing me a postcard showing what looked like a tiny fishing village but which I recognized as a spot along the bay not far from City Hall. "He told me that when he grew up, he was going to bring me all the calamari I wanted."

Elder Grant turned up his nose. The mission rules insisted we eat anything placed before us and never make a single negative comment no matter what. The only exception was if someone tried to serve us coffee or wine. Despite growing up in New Orleans, I'd never been a big fan of seafood other than catfish. Catfish were great. But I'd had calamari twice since coming to Italy. It wasn't the delight others seemed to think it was, but it wasn't awful, either. I knew my companion had never even been offered the dish before. His turned up nose was just his gut reaction.

The way people felt about froci like us.

"Here's one of Castel Sant'Elmo," she said. "We had so much fun pretending it was our secret fortress." Elisabetta showed us two dozen more postcards, mostly of local sights, where she and her son had spent happy times. The last one in the box revealed a large but not particularly impressive church.

"It's where we went to mass," Sister Coticelli said. For the first time that evening, she looked wistful. "Enea stopped coming with me after his father disappeared." She'd handed each of the other postcards to us one by one to let us view them more carefully. This one she kept on her lap.

"We sent Enea's name to the temple in Switzerland," I told her, "like we said we'd do." I'd explained on a previous visit that Bern was the closest temple Italian Mormons had access to. We didn't pray for the dead the way Catholics did, so I was telling a white lie. Elder Grant and I had sent Elisabetta's name, not her son's, to be put on the prayer roll.

Near the end of every temple ceremony, several people from the audience would get up and form a prayer circle, interlocking their hands with secret handshakes as they petitioned Heavenly Father to bless the people whose names were on the list.

But I knew as soon as I mentioned the prayer roll that I'd messed up. "Elisabetta," I said, trying to correct myself, "what would *you* like us to do for Enea?"

She frowned and stared at my tie for a long moment. My stake president back home had forbidden me to bring my *Star Trek* tie clip to Italy. I just wore boring ties every day with no clips or pins of any kind. Elder Murdock had mentioned we could get a Moroni cameo tie clip made special here, but I'd already gone through my extra $20 for the month, plus another. And Moroni wasn't as exciting as Spock.

Elder Grant and I had visited Elisabetta on three other occasions, but this was the first time she'd shown us the postcards. Yet she still didn't seem ready to trust us.

"Would you like us to light a candle at that church?" I indicated the postcard she still held in her lap. We couldn't let the other elders know, of course, but then, we were becoming le mani vecchie at keeping secrets.

She nodded timidly and then opened her mouth without speaking.

"Something else?" I asked.

"Anziani," she said, looking now at the photos on her wall, "can you pray the rosary with me?"

I felt Elder Grant stiffen beside me on the sofa.

"We don't know how," I said, leaning forward slightly, hoping I didn't sound as stupid as I felt, "but if you'll teach us, we'll be happy to."

***

Neither Elder Grant nor I was in the mood for 24-hour work. It was always hard getting back into the proselyting mood on Mondays. We climbed off the bus in front of the building where the solitary branch of the Church used to meet on Via Roma until the earthquake last November. The building had survived but was too badly damaged for us to stay. Instead, the branch relocated to the conference room on the top floor of a ten-story hotel in the most modern part of town, where new construction replaced previous structures. The city was two thousand years old. No one was going to find any virgin land.

The hotel was the exact same height as the apartment building on Via Stadera that had collapsed during the quake. Over twenty-six hundred people had been killed in the region altogether, maybe up to five thousand, most in smaller towns to our south and east. Dozens of children in an orphanage were crushed, families having dinner at home, worshippers in an old Catholic church, young people making out in cars on a small-town Lovers' Lane.

The elders in Castellammare were right in the middle of a baptismal service in their apartment when the building started falling apart all around them. They slept on the beach that night.

The man never did get baptized.

I wasn't in Napoli at the time, but the missionaries who were all reported steep drops in their weekly stats for the next few months. Both the elders in Castellammare and those in Napoli 1 had to find new apartments, plus the zone leaders had been charged with locating another location for the branch to meet.

The top floor of the hotel was the only truly nice place I'd seen since coming to the city, with two walls made of glass allowing us a grand view sometimes more inspiring than either the talks or the lessons.

Yesterday before services, I'd watched as Sister Pulzella smiled and thrust her 17-year-old daughter in front of Elder Snow, who'd just been transferred into Napoli 3, the district adjacent to ours. "She'll be old enough to marry by the time you finish your mission," she said. "Why don't you young people talk for a moment while I ask Sorella Scarfato about next week's lesson?"

"I'm sorry about my mother," the girl said after her mother walked off, but it still looked like she had to restrain herself from holding onto Elder Snow's arm and pulling him aside for a more private chat.

Most of the members in Napoli were true converts. That didn't mean, of course, they didn't recognize an opportunity when they saw one. For some, this was their only chance to negotiate marriage to an American. For others less concerned about nationality, it was still one of their limited chances simply to arrange for a temple wedding.

While the Napoli branch was far larger than any of the branches in Cagliari or Rome, reducing the strain of hearing the same speakers over and over, there were days I still found it difficult to drag myself to the meetings. Of course, attendance wasn't optional. Neither was paying attention. Elder Murdock often quizzed us after services about what we'd heard.

Fortunately, the Sacrament meeting on Sunday started off with a hymn I'd loved ever since childhood. "O Creature del Signor" by St. Francis of Assisi. The words and rhymes worked much better in Italian than English, and the song was already lovely in English. The poem on which it was based had been one of the earliest religious texts written in the vernacular, in this case the Umbrian dialect, but we weren't singing in Umbrian. For my first several months in Italy, every day seemed an exercise in overcoming culture shock. These days, though, I kept discovering wonderful things I realized I'd never have experienced if I hadn't come on a mission.

Church talks, unfortunately, were pretty much the same everywhere. One of those given yesterday was on the difference between obeying the spirit of the law versus the letter of the law. Another was on the power of prayer. And the last was on the importance of paying our tithing.

I passed Elder Murdock's quiz over lunch after we got home.

But I'd kept looking past the speakers and through the wall of glass behind them, paying only partial attention. Vesuvius always incited conflicting feelings of comfort and melancholy, a familiar face in a city where every time I turned a corner, I felt lost.

As Elder Grant and I roamed around listlessly on another sultry Monday morning, I noticed the spot on Piazza Dante where a huge bell had crushed Brother Esposito's car during the quake. I watched as throngs of passengers surged onto a bus, three hanging on to the doors as the vehicle took off. I saw elderly women placing candles and other offerings in front of small shrines set up ages ago throughout the city. Some local festival I was unaware of had engaged two dozen old men to carry a portrait of Mary in a glass box while a handful of schoolchildren in red sashes played a few instruments as only schoolchildren could. On another street, we saw a broken statue of Mary set up in front of an old church. The bottom half of Mary was still in place after last fall's quake, but Mary from the waist up was propped beside the front doors to the chapel, with fresh flowers set all around her.

"Buon giorno," I said with a half-hearted smile to a man walking by. He kept on toward his destination.

"Buona giornata," I tried with another man fifteen minutes later. He looked at me, frowned, and kept walking.

We'd lost the Spirit.

We were wasting our time. I was wasting my father's money.

I was wasting Elder Grant's life.

In the past week, my companion and I had shot off into each other's yogurt cups and blended the two substances for late morning treats. Yogurt here was a thick liquid rather than the harder, gelatinous mass it was in America. I'd put honey on Elder Grant's asshole and licked it off. He'd put Nutella on my nipples and licked that off. Elder Grant had shot into a large spoon and fed me some "medicina dei colleghi." I kept thinking about Lucy Ricardo's reaction to Vitameatavegamin. While cum was an acquired taste, it grew more intoxicating every single day.

Still, when I was using Elder Grant's cum as lube on my dick to jack off, and then he in turn used my cum to jack himself off a second time, I couldn't help worrying that the things we were doing might be *more* sinful than straight-out sex.

"Let's try the ghetto," Elder Grant suggested after a while. "People are always a little more humble there." The first time I ventured into the centro storico sparked the revelation that "ghetto" was an Italian word.

But even among the humble, we still didn't feel like talking to anyone. I noticed the carts and tables set up to sell slightly damaged umbrellas, to sell used bras, to sell worn-out shoes. An old man perched at a sewing machine took tailoring orders. A middle-aged woman sold live chickens locked up in a tiny pen. Several men had tables set up to sell cartons of cigarettes. Laundry hung from half the balconies in sight, some lines strung across the street between buildings.

Of course, even in middle-class neighborhoods, people hung out their laundry to dry. Back in Quartu, we'd used a spare room in our apartment for the task. Here in Napoli 2, we had a dryer in the bathroom next to the washing machine.

A Vespa scooted past us, the teenage driver flicking a cigarette butt into a tray of blood oranges.

Wouldn't it be great if the Napoli branch could adopt three or four blocks in the centro storico as a Service Project and clean them regularly?

Preposterous, I realized, watching as a vendor a few stalls up the street threw a tomato at the Vespa driver long since out of range, an act of solidarity rather than justice.

There were only 12,000 Latter-day Saints in all of Italy, no more than 110 who met each week here. 110 out of over two million Napoletani. Not even the zone leaders had baptized anyone since I'd arrived, though the sisters in Pozzuolli had baptized a young woman two weeks ago.

Well, the sisters had taught the woman but, of course, one of the elders was the one to baptize her.

Elder Grant stopped in front of a table where a portly man was selling magazines. Pornographic magazines.

"Anziano," I said.

"It's all women." He sounded disappointed. "No men."

"We could hardly buy them anyway," I said.

"I know, but…"

I waited.

He shrugged. "Don't you get tired of being invisible?" He shrugged again. "It's like…I don't know…it's like being told we don't exist."

I sometimes felt that way as a non-Utah Mormon. The other missionaries often said things like, "How nice that they let converts come to the important missions" or "They made a convert like your father a councilor in the bishopric after only three years?" My family had converted when I was four. I'd never known any other religion. I'd been Seminary class president twice, the Deacons' Quorum president, the Teachers' Quorum president, and the First Assistant to the bishop, since the bishop himself was always the Priests' Quorum president.

"Sometimes, when people won't even look us in the eye, I start to wonder if I'm really even here." He locked eyes with mine. "I start thinking maybe I'm insane."

Matto. Pazzo. The words were almost interchangeable. While my companion contemplated his mental stability, at times like this, what I was always struck by was how normal life in Italy had become for me. Italians, at least, saw me as a real Mormon. I thought nothing of going into a "bar" and grabbing a triangle or two of milk. Friends back home would write and ask if I expected to ever be able to think in Italian, as if that were some near monumental feat. But I'd been thinking in Italian ever since my first district.

It was just like thinking in English, after all. Maybe at first you only knew the word "door." But then you learned the words for "entrance" and "exit" and "sliding glass door" and "screen door" and "revolving door." And when you thought in English, you just thought the word most appropriate to the situation. When I saw a door in Italy, I didn't have to think "door" and then translate it. I just thought "porta" or "portone" or "entrata" or "uscita" or whatever other variation was best suited to the visual stimulus my brain was receiving.

When I saw the stand of magazines Elder Grant was staring at, I didn't think "magazines." I thought, "Oh, una tavola piena di riviste. Riviste pornografiche." Thinking in Italian wasn't an accomplishment. It was unavoidable. And if I didn't know a particular word necessary to complete a certain thought, I didn't struggle. I just inserted the English word needed without any need to "change gears." I might struggle a bit when speaking, since circumlocution required such careful analysis, but I had no need for circumlocution when I thought.

"You remember that porn magazine, *Oui*?" I asked.

"Sí."

"When I was a kid, some of the other boys in the neighborhood found a copy of the magazine, and we all looked at it in my friend Howard's treehouse." I'd been infatuated with Howard for years. There was a vacant lot next to his house where his father had built him the treehouse. He called it his Batcave, since he was as big a fan of Adam West as I was. His mother also let him run around in just a loincloth when we played cowboys and Indians. I knew not to tell my mother that detail or she'd never have let me play with Howard again. And I wanted to play with Howard.

He ended up getting arrested a couple of times as a teenager for drug use. I hadn't seen him since I was sixteen.

"I don't think I've ever looked at porn," Elder Grant said in a melancholy tone.

"If this helps illustrate just how gay I am," I said, "out of that entire magazine, the only image I can remember is the title, *Oui*." I smiled, and a moment later, Elder Grant began to chuckle.

"One of these days," he said, "I'm going to take a *good* picture of *you*."

I didn't need to translate to know what "good" meant. Or that a life-size image of the part of my body he was referring to by "you" would fit all too easily on 4x6 photo stock.

We continued wandering through the streets, not talking to anyone but no longer feeling purposeless. We ducked into one building to try some day tracting. The stairwell was supported by heavy beams we had to dodge to climb up.

The consequences of sin.

On the first floor, a young man about our age answered the door. "Ciao," he said with a big smile, making the sign of the cross. "I was praying for help, and here you are."

Eccovi. Back in Sardinia, on my first day in church, the branch president had asked me, "Can you…?" and then made the sign of the cross. I'd been shocked until I realized he was only asking if I knew how to direct music.

"I just got up off my knees," the young man continued, shaking his head in wonder. "My mamma told me God always answers sincere pleas for help."

We *were* still following the promptings of the Holy Ghost!

"Can we come in?" asked Elder Grant.

"Certo, certo." The young man ushered us inside. The place was small, naturally. While not dirty, and even if the sparse furniture could only have been a few years old, the place felt ancient, like we'd stumbled across a hand-me-down sofa in a lighted cave. For a moment, I couldn't quite put my finger on what was wrong but then realized the walls weren't smooth and flat, instead looking as if someone had hand-plastered them two hundred years ago.

Posters of soccer players and male pop stars decorated the walls. Plus, a poster of two shirtless men, one man with his hand on the other man's shoulder.

My initial reaction was that I'd had a prayer of my own answered. But then I remembered Italian men were less threatened by physical touch than Americans. The branch president in Cagliari used to kiss me on the forehead. The two guys on the poster were probably just bandmates or something. I'd felt the Spirit the first time I'd noticed two young men holding hands in Quartu. As I looked at the photograph now, the Holy Ghost witnessed to me that *this* was one of the reasons Heavenly Father had sent a convert to an "important mission."

Elder Grant introduced himself, motioned for me to do the same, and then asked the young man his name. "Mi chiamo Antonio," he said. Then he called over his shoulder. "Stefano! Venga!"

A moment later, another young man strode out of the bedroom wearing nothing but a towel. He walked over and sat beside Antonio.

"How long have you guys been together?" Antonio asked.

So maybe I wasn't witnessing normal Italian affection between men.

But I still felt the Spirit.

"This is only our second month," Elder Grant replied. "My previous companion got transferred to Ostia, and Anziano Mortensen came down from Ciampino." He smiled and patted me on the knee. "He's the best companion I've ever had."

Antonio and Stefano exchanged glances. Even I was surprised at how obtuse Elder Grant seemed to be.

Italian was such an easy language. One could even guess that "ottuso" was the right word, once you knew a few of the rules.

"We've been lovers for about a year," Antonio said. He leaned over and gave Stefano a long, slow kiss. When he faced us again, he said, "Our anniversary's coming up next week. I was wondering what to get him." He squeezed Stefano's arm. "We can't afford much." He looked about the room. "But then you guys showed up."

"Oh!" Elder Grant exclaimed, jumping to his feet. "I think you guys—I think—"

"What can we do for you?" I asked calmly.

Elder Grant swirled his head around to stare at me.

"A fourway?" Antonio suggested with a shrug. "A threeway? Swap partners?"

"Mannaggia la miseria!" Elder Grant almost shouted.

I took my companion's hand and dragged him back to his seat. "I'm not sure any of that will work," I said. But really, I thought, would licking Stefano's asshole be any more of a sin than licking Elder Grant's? It would still merely be helping him get in the mood to masturbate. I wouldn't be having intercourse with him. Elder Grant's asshole wasn't sealed to me in the temple any more than Stefano's.

And what harm could there be, really, in having Elder Grant jack off into his own hand in the presence of these other men before I licked it up? It was the exact same thing we did in our room alone. Did the act change in any meaningful way because we had an audience? It was either a sin or it wasn't.

Well, of course it was a sin. But it wouldn't be any *bigger* a sin with a couple of onlookers.

I stood up and started taking off my tie.

"Anziano Mortensen!" My companion pointed at me with the same expression Donald Sutherland had when he pointed at Veronica Cartwright during the conclusion of *Invasion of the Body Snatchers*.

"Is it any help to you guys," I asked, "if we take off our clothes and get hard while we watch you two have sex?"

Stefano jumped to his feet and ripped off his towel. Antonio stood more slowly but with a broader smile as he pulled off his T-shirt. I began unbuttoning my carefully ironed shirt as well and motioned for my companion to join in. He frowned, looked about in bewilderment, and then stood and disrobed alongside me. We were both fully and painfully erect long before our garments came off.

Antonio and Stefano stopped groping each other for a moment and looked us over. "Cavolo!" Antonio said.

Didn't that mean cabbage? Elder Grant and I really did need to study the language even more and our missionary lessons a little less. I'd only taught a J once in the past year. Why did I need to spend so much time making sure I kept it memorized?

"I think you guys are gods," Stefano said breathlessly.

"Oh, no," Elder Grant protested. "Not until after Judgment Day."

I watched as Stefano grabbed a can of vegetable shortening, applied some to his dick and another dab to Antonio's ass, and then slowly slid all the way inside him. I immediately felt the Spirit testifying to me yet again of the importance of proxy work in the temple. Sometimes, it took something concrete to understand something abstract. There was no reason the Lord couldn't use sin to illustrate truth. We all learned something from Adam and Eve eating the forbidden fruit. We all learned something from King David lusting after Bathsheba. And sometimes, we needed those lessons over and over to fully appreciate them.

It was a shame I'd never be able to use my new insight in a Sacrament talk, even if it stopped others from daydreaming while they looked at the view through the window.

I smiled as Stefano pulled his long dick almost all the way out of Antonio's ass before sliding it all the way back in. Stefano groaned and Antonio grunted. I remembered watching a construction crew building a house near the stake center in Metairie, a pile driver slamming a piling again and again until it finally sank deep enough into the Earth to act as a foundation. Once, Stefano's dick slipped out completely when he pulled back too far, and they both groaned when he pushed it right back through Antonio's sphincter as deep as it would go.

I really hadn't meant to take part, but I ejaculated onto Stefano's back while Elder Grant shot into Antonio's face.

But we never touched either man. It wasn't as if we'd had an orgy or anything like President Alsop warned they used to do in Pompeii.

Afterward, we wished the two young men a happy anniversary and pulled our clothes back on. It was almost time to head back to the apartment for lunch.

I paused in the stairwell, my hand on one of the heavy beams.

"Ouch!" I said. "I got a damn splinter."

Chapter Six:
The Three Nephites

The bus up the hill was crowded as usual, and Elder Grant and I found ourselves shoved into the rear left-hand corner. The back portion of the bus had no seats, making it easier to cram more riders in once the seats toward the middle and front of the bus were occupied and the aisles filled.

I held my flip charts and Book of Mormon against my side while Elder Grant held the tracting book in which we logged each address where we'd knocked on doors. In the commotion of boarding, a short, heavyset woman in black hit me behind the knee with a plastic shopping bag just after we took off. I buckled and fell against my companion.

"Mi scusi," the middle-aged woman offered without much conviction.

"Certo," I replied, unable to regain my footing in the crowd.

"Stay right there, Anziano," Elder Grant whispered in my ear. "I like your head on my shoulder." He inhaled deeply. "Your hair smells so good."

"Well, *my* nose is right next to your arm pit," I pointed out.

"And?"

"And your deodorant is holding up just fine." I paused just a moment and then added, "Tomorrow, you might try using a little less, and we'll see how that goes."

He stroked my hair briefly with his free hand. A teenage girl beside him snickered. Then she grinned and said, "I speek Eeenglish," haltingly in such a thick accent I suspected it was the only English phrase she knew. But she followed it up a moment later with, "Reagan bad," as if trying to prove just how much she understood about the world. I'd been kicked twice in Quartu by teens who disliked America. A man in Rome had spit on me, muttering something about American imperialism.

Elder Grant hadn't been there to lick it off.

What was wrong with me?

We were standard bearers for the Lord, and it was clear Elder Grant and I couldn't present a good example, much less talk about the Church, while we sniffed each other in public like Neapolitan mastiffs. I stood up straight again, accidentally nudging the woman with the plastic shopping bags with my elbow.

"Mi scusi," I said.

***

One afternoon, Elder Grant and I left the apartment after lunch concluded at 3:30, and we waited around the corner until the other two companionships departed. The ZLs didn't leave until almost 4:00.

We ducked back inside for a quick jack off session, but while Elder Grant's zucchini was still up my ass, we heard someone unlock the front door.

"You call Brother Tartaglione," Elder Murdock told his companion. "Io devo pisciare."

But he paused at the bathroom door without going in. Instead, he walked to the end of the hallway. We could hear his footsteps stopping right outside our door.

We were afraid even to breathe, but surely, he could still hear our hearts pounding. The neighbors could probably hear.

A few seconds later—an eternity—the footsteps retreated down the hall back toward the bathroom. Elder Grant and I didn't move for another ten minutes until the zone leaders locked the front door again on their way out.

We spent the rest of our jack off session massaging our cramped muscles.

***

"What a great morning," Elder Grant said as we walked out of the apartment building we'd just tracted. "Both parents were home, *and* their three kids. We got to teach the whole family an *entire* lesson." He did a little dance, even though it was forbidden. "We could be baptizing *five* people soon." That would be almost triple the annual baptismal rate for any elder in our mission. Elder Grant had already baptized two people in previous districts. I had yet to baptize anyone.

Colloquio C detailing Joseph Smith's First Vision was still the only missionary lesson I knew word for word all the way through, the only lesson out of eight we taught with any consistency. There were no A or B discussions, though there must have been at some point.

This was the first time I'd even wondered what they'd covered.

"The Di Martinos are even having us back next Saturday for the D." Elder Grant patted me on the back. I wasn't sure if he was happy for the Di Martinos or for us, if he saw our success as a sign of Heavenly Father's favor.

"The Plan of Salvation," I said. I could usually get up to speed on that one in a couple of hours. I felt happy, too, but I wasn't sure of my motivations, either. Could a person have a conflict of interest if the "reward" wasn't tangible?

Elder Grant looked absentmindedly at his left hand, wiggling his ring finger.

I checked my watch. "We don't have time to get back to the apartment for lunch."

"Dannazione." Elder Grant frowned. "I can't keep working till 9:30 without food." He was no longer looking at his left hand, but his ring finger was still flicking back and forth as if trying to take flight.

"Why don't we grab some fruit and eat in the park?" I pointed to a tiny storefront with crates of produce out front.

We grabbed some red grapes, declining the vendor's suggestion we buy some bosc pears and blood oranges as well, and then ducked into the neighboring store for two small chunks of provolone. At a shop next to that one, we picked up a loaf of pane cafone.

Just inside Parco Viviani, we stood a few yards off from a bench occupied by an elderly man and waited to see if he would move on in a few minutes.

He didn't.

I wondered if I could talk my companion into lying on the ground in his dress pants and white shirt while I fed him. Maybe I could lay my flip charts down first so he wouldn't get his clothes dirty. Perhaps afterward, I could rest my head on his chest while we rehearsed our discussions.

"Come on," Elder Grant told me, "there's room for all of us." We approached the bench, and Elder Grant nodded at the older gentleman, who looked a bit like Totó. My companion and I had watched a bit of *I soliti ignoti* with a member family once. "Vuoi un pezzo di pane?" Elder Grant held up the round loaf of bread.

The man smiled and scooted to the far end of the bench. Elder Grant sat beside him, tearing off a piece of the cafone, and I sat next to my companion.

"Grazie mille," the old man replied, ripping out a portion from the loaf and shoving it into his mouth.

According to the wrinkles and slightly pungent odor, he'd been wearing the same clothes for three or four days.

I thought about my companion's dried cum on the garments under my pillow waiting for me at bedtime tonight.

"You live near here?" Elder Grant asked him.

Not likely. Vomero was a more comfortable neighborhood than even we could afford. Nothing like Posillipo, but pleasant.

The old man pointed vaguely to our right.

I wasn't terribly interested in getting a referral, however, irritated to be sharing my companion with him or anyone else during our special lunch. As individual missionaries, we rarely had any time completely to ourselves other than five minutes a day in the bathroom, if we were lucky. But I was finally in a place where I *enjoyed* being with my companion twenty-four hours a day. That certainly wasn't the case in previous districts, even with companions I liked. Now I realized that a companionship rarely had any time away from other elders, either, since so many of us shared the same apartment. And when we were out of the house, we were among hordes of other people. I understood that part of the reason six of us lived together was to save on costs, that another part was to offer emotional support to one another, but of course I also realized a significant part of the motivation was to make it harder for missionaries to sin. And since I wanted to sin, I found the situation intolerable.

Yet there was really nothing I could do but tolerate it. I bit off half a large grape, chewed it while picking out the seeds visible in the remaining portion, and then slid that half into my mouth as well.

Fresh grapes were good, but no match for my companion's attention.

"Do you like your neighborhood?" Elder Grant continued.

Don't, don't, don't, *don't* try to get his address, I begged him telepathically.

"Been there seventy-five years," the man said. "Born there and I'll die there."

I couldn't fully make out every word, as much of it was either in Napoletano or just uttered with a thick Napoletan accent.

The man took another bite of bread, closing his eyes as if he'd just tasted a high-quality Pandoro.

"What's your favorite food?" Elder Grant asked.

I considered tapping my companion's shoe with mine. I realized this was almost the same question I'd asked of Elisabetta on our first meeting, and the fact that this irritated me was irritating. Being nice to strangers was one thing, but we were off the clock at lunchtime. Couldn't we relax for just a few minutes? I was tired of being "on" all the time.

No wonder the Three Nephites went around incognito.

The old man swallowed his mouthful and looked at Elder Grant, leaning forward then to get a better look at me, too. "Spaghetti alle vongole," he said. He peered at our books as if searching for a container of pasta or clams.

"Is it just you and your wife at home?"

"Sono vedovo."

"Oh," Elder Grant said softly. "I'm sorry to hear that."

The old man shrugged and pulled his remaining portion of bread up to his nose to breathe in its fragrance.

"How about we stop by tomorrow evening and bring dinner with us? Do you mind the company?"

The man frowned, his eyes flitting back and forth between my companion and me. "No, no," he said. "Venite, venite."

Elder Grant pulled out a pen and asked for the address. The man gave us another searching look and then told us his street and house number. Definitely sounded like something in the centro storico.

The old man looked a little confused when Elder Grant put away his notepad and offered his hand. Then the gentleman stood up as if to go but hesitated. Elder Grant handed him a small bunch of grapes from our bag. The man took them, nodded, and walked off. It was only then that I realized what the conversation had been for.

Another conflict of interest.

"That was an expensive way to get the bench to ourselves," I said. But it was certainly gentle. I wanted to kiss Elder Grant on the lips.

He shrugged. "It's not expensive in the least, Elder Mortensen. Not for me, anyway. I'll have *you* pay for the vongole." He grinned. "Besides, I think all three of us will enjoy the meal tomorrow night."

"Since you'll be there," I said, "non c'é dubbio."

I realized we didn't even know the old man's name.

Elder Grant grinned again and popped a grape into his mouth. He leaned toward me, pushing the grape to the edge of his lips with his tongue. I leaned forward and sucked the tiny red ball into my mouth.

The seeds were crunchy and a little bitter, but I swallowed them anyway.

***

My mother's Patriarchal Blessing assured her my father would always be faithful. The fact that Heavenly Father felt she needed this reassurance had always left me unsettled. *I* would never be unfaithful, I vowed, and my wife would *know* she'd never need worry.

And yet at the first opportunity, I'd gotten naked with Antonio and Stefano. Still, since Anziano Grant had been there as well, it couldn't truly be described as cheating. Especially since neither of us had even touched either of the other men in a sexual way.

With our history of polygamy, the subject of multiple sex partners was never filed away completely. My issue had only been hoping that one day the Church would allow monogamy between men. Or would that be monoandry? Polyandry seemed an idea too extreme. Knowing Joseph Smith had practiced it, though, had given me a tiny hope that someday, maybe even before the Millennium, some form of gay marriage might be allowed.

The evening after we met the two young men, I added something new to my evening masturbation session with Elder Grant.

"Once," I whispered after Lights Out, "a guy from my ward was taking a hike in the woods in Mississippi. He'd never been a Boy Scout and got lost."

Elder Grant's hand caressed my knee.

"After two days, he started getting weak from hunger. He didn't know that many parts of a pine tree are edible."

My companion chuckled at the allusion to Euell Gibbons.

"He was able to drink from a stream, but he kept getting weaker, and he finally leaned against a tree, waiting to die." Elder Grant stopped caressing my knee. "Then three other men showed up. They were dressed like hunters, but no one had a gun. One of them kneeled down in front of the man, straddled him, and put his dick in the man's mouth."

"Mannaggia."

"The hunter told him he was there to make sure the lost hiker received adequate protein to survive." Elder Grant gripped my knee tightly and held on. "One by one, each of the three men shot a healthy load of protein into the starving man's mouth. They stayed with him and fed him again and again every couple of hours until he regained enough strength to keep walking. He eventually found a road and lived to tell the tale." The accounts that some of the older folks related during Fast and Testimony meeting might have made the rest of the congregation uncomfortable, but even those with the most advanced dementia would never have told such a story.

"The Three Nephites." Elder Grant breathed out heavily. When it dawned on him the story was made up, he hit me playfully in the arm. "You flipper."

"What else are they going to do?" I asked. "Have sex with random women for two thousand years? For them to maintain any level of chastity, they'd have to have sex with each other."

"And the occasional hiker."

"Well, that's just a mission of mercy." Oh, to be called to a service mission instead of a proselyting one.

"Mannaggia!" my companion grabbed my knee again. "Tell me about another mission of mercy."

And so we began telling each other Three Nephite stories at bedtime. An old man's car might get a flat tire out in the desert. The man would be stressed and scared, so after the Three Nephites changed his tire, they also found a way to relieve the man's stress. "While the First Nephite sucks the old man off, the Second Nephite fucks the old man in the ass, and the old man sucks off the Third Nephite."

Naturally, there was a limit to how precisely we could act out the stories, but we tried to get as close as possible. Perhaps Elder Grant couldn't penetrate me, but he could shoot into my crack. Then he'd take his fingers and gently push as much of his cum as possible into my asshole. Rather than having my companion suck me off, I'd shoot toward his open mouth. Whatever didn't make it inside might hit his cheek or chin, and I'd lick that part off.

A man's chin wasn't a sex organ.

Neither was an armpit. Sometimes, I'd ask my companion to skip applying deodorant right after showering before bedtime. He was still relatively clean, but there was now just a hint of earthiness added to the taste of his skin that lasted all night. He still insisted on applying at least a thin layer before we left the apartment the following morning, but if I huddled close enough to him on the bus ride home, I could feel its protection fading in the summer heat, and I might then pretend to stumble to get a closer whiff.

Mostly, though, because our bedtime stories involved a third man, it was impossible even to come close to performing a successful proxy threeway. So we'd just gently stroke ourselves as we added onto the story of the evening, improvising as we went. "The First Nephite is sucking the Second Nephite's dick," I might say. "And the

Third Nephite licks the side of the asshole where the cock keeps going in and out. And when the First Nephite cums and pulls his dick out of the Second Nephite's ass, a little cum drips out, too, and the Third Nephite licks it up."

"Then the Third Nephite puts his dick in the Second Nephite's mouth," Elder Grant might add, "and the First Nephite licks the saliva dripping out of the side of the Second Nephite's mouth as his face is getting fucked. Then when the Third Nephite cums and pulls his dick out of the Second Nephite's mouth, a little cum drips out and the First Nephite licks that up, too."

If two men could engage in a large variety of sexual acts, three men could find even more things to do. Of course, Elder Grant and I weren't having sex ourselves. We were just talking about it, and words weren't sex.

We didn't fantasize about the Three Nephites every evening, naturally. One night after Lights Out, we gave each other priesthood blessings. Instead of anointing with the consecrated olive oil stored in the vials on our keychains, though, we anointed with our cum. It didn't feel sacrilegious, the same way that traditional sexual intercourse might seem a decadent sin two days before a temple wedding and yet two days *after* a temple wedding became a glorious, God-approved act of love. Since Elder Grant and I weren't touching each other's penis, anointing one another's head with cum was just love, not sex.

The day we made it past another Transfer meeting, Elder Grant and I toasted the accomplishment by both shooting our cum into the same glass of water, then adding the thick almond syrup used in Italian sodas. I took a sip, then he took a sip, then I took a sip, then he took another, until the glass was empty.

It was better than being blood brothers. That was kid stuff.

Tonight, we told three Three Nephite stories, the same event narrated from three different perspectives. It was almost torture to wait until the end to orgasm. We both shot into the same bowl and took turns mixing it with our index fingers. Then Elder Grant scooped up about half of our combined cum and put it on my ass as I lay face down. "How do I love thee?" he asked. "Let me count the ways." Corny when I first heard it in high school, and exquisite when I heard it now.

"I love the way you block the men at bus stops until all the women can board."

"I love the way you hand out milk candies to the kids at church."

"I love the way you help Elder Murdock with the dishes even when it's his turn, to give him a chance to vent about the things he won't tell his companion."

"And I love the way you won't tell me anything he says."

With each comment my companion made, he pushed a little more cum past my sphincter, over and over until he could get no more in. After licking his fingers, he lay face down, and I pushed the rest of our cum into his ass, telling him all the ways I loved him, too.

Chapter Seven:
Dancing to Pirate Music

Elder Grant and I had returned to Lovers' Lane the previous evening, where we held hands as we watched tiny Cinquecentos across the street bouncing up and down. Eventually, just watching began to feel a bit unfulfilling, so we took the next step and urinated together onto some used hypodermics in the gutter.

A teenage boy who couldn't have been over fifteen staggered down the road carrying a nearly empty bottle of wine. It probably wasn't his first of the evening. He leaned against a stone wall only a few feet from one of the cars, unzipped, and beat off with one hand while occasionally lifting the bottle to his lips with the other.

"Remember when Sister Coticelli used that phrase, 'Avere la botte piena e la moglie ubriaca'?" I asked.

"Have a full bottle and a drunk wife," Elder Grant said.

"I just realized what it means." Have your cake and eat it, too.

Elder Grant tore his eyes away from the rocking cars and looked at me with a frown.

"Can we have our physical intimacy," I asked, "and our virginity, too?"

Spaccamoralitá. Missionaries made up fake Italian words all the time.

A commotion across the street caught our attention. A young man in the car where the teen was beating off had discovered the voyeur a few feet away. He burst out of the car, pulled up his unzipped pants, and started smacking the teen over the head. Too drunk to defend himself, the boy curled down onto the street, where the young man continued to hit and kick him until his girlfriend dragged him back into the car, which began to rock more vigorously than before.

I'd never been impressed with Lou Ferrigno's body, but the reason hadn't been a mystery. Anger wasn't pretty. It was always disappointing to run into decent people who might have made good members of the Church but who wouldn't be baptized because they were always so angry at God. Eternal spiritual Hulks.

Bill Bixby, on the other hand…

I'd first fallen in love with him when I was six years old, sitting in the back seat of our family car at the drive-in watching *Clambake*. Mom loved Elvis Presley, but Bill Bixby was the boy-next-door hero of the movie for me.

A tornado had taken out that screen later, just as the closing credits were rolling on the last film the theater was scheduled to show before shutting down for good.

"Look," I said, pointing to the merchandise on display at one of the tables in the open market. We were out this afternoon to purchase more vongole for yet another dinner with Luigi, the elderly man whose park bench we'd stolen. Turned out he was a nice old man we enjoyed visiting.

Except for his anger at God.

It wasn't God's fault his wife had a stroke and was confined to her bed for the last year of her life. It wasn't God's fault Antonella had begged Luigi to put her out of her misery.

There was no point telling anyone Luigi had used a pillow.

He served us sour, curdled milk each time we visited, all he had to offer.

Murderers on TV were never nice.

"It's San Gennaro," Elder Grant said, looking toward the small statuette. The patron saint of Napoli, who'd stopped the lava from reaching the city and destroying it. Some of his blood in a vial liquified every year, testifying to his continued protection.

"É il tuo compleanno fra due giorni," I said. "I'm buying it for you."

"Oh, Elder, I don't need a Catholic saint for my birthday."

I'd seen open markets in the French Quarter back home, but they were only half directed to the local populace. Most of the goods were targeted for tourists: T-shirts with slogans like "Laissez les bons temps rouler" or "Throw me something, mister!"; perhaps coffee mugs featuring a drunk alligator catching beads or a drunk man urinating on a Bourbon Street lamp post. But virtually everything in Napoli seemed to be aimed at everyday citizens. I'd bought socks and a couple of ties. I'd bought a floral ceramic tile to send my mother for her anniversary. Sure, a tourist might buy a statue of San Gennaro, but so would a lot of the locals.

"It'll be a reminder of how being together in Napoli helped us stop before we did any real damage." I picked up the small statue to inspect it further.

Elder Grant frowned. "How about," he countered, "on my birthday, we do some real damage?"

I froze. "Wh-what did you have in mind?"

My companion leaned over and whispered in my ear. "Why don't you slide inside me?" he asked. "But don't fuck me. That's *too* much spiritual damage. But you could…"

"Sí?"

"Why don't you slide your dick up my ass," he said, "and piss inside me?"

I dropped the statuette. The vendor started yelling and waving his arms about wildly as if I'd just chopped off his toe. I quickly picked San Gennaro up off the street and pulled out my wallet.

"Pissing isn't having sex," Elder Grant said. "Urine isn't semen."

"Flip!"

He paused a moment. "Anziano?" His brows furrowed. "Anziano?"

"I'm not sure I can wait two days to celebrate your birthday."

A few stalls down, we ran into Sister Longobardi selling a variety of fresh flowers. We chatted about Relief Society, about her husband who had vowed never to convert, and how she hoped one day when her daughter was a little older, she could send the girl off to Utah to find a good man.

Our hands were already overflowing with our scriptures and flip charts and statue, but I felt obligated to buy a few flowers and so chose half a dozen daisies. Elisabetta didn't live all that far from Luigi.

"Ci vediamo la domenica!" Sister Longobardi said with a smile, throwing in an extra flower.

We started making our way back toward Spaccanapoli. We hadn't walked more than a few feet, though, before we saw a young boy scamper off with a tweed ivy cap he'd grabbed off another table. The vendor, a spry older woman, leaped after him with what I'd assumed was her cane but which turned out to be the tool she used to go after thieves. She struck the boy on the head, he dropped the cap, and she placed it back on her table with no more irritation than if she'd just swatted a fly from her dinner.

"All in a day's work," I said, laughing. Elder Grant didn't laugh, but then, my joke wasn't all that funny. He stopped walking and I put my hand on his shoulder. "You okay?"

"I thought about shoplifting once," he said softly.

"Yes?" I'd never felt any such desire. Still, it didn't seem like a big deal. He'd only thought about it, after all. I'd thought about drinking a glass of wine once during Transfers.

"I was sixteen," he continued. "I was hoping, I don't know, to get at least half a day of jail out of it. Juvenile detention, anyway."

"No offense, Anziano, but I don't picture you as the rebel type."

"I rehearsed telling the judge not to be lenient, that I needed to be scared straight."

I remembered the documentary.

"I was hoping to get fucked in detention, maybe by a guard or two, hopefully by five or six other delinquents. I used to stay awake for an hour, night after night, fantasizing and planning."

I put my hand on his arm. There was so much I still didn't know about this man. Yes, he'd told me stories about joining the Donny and Marie fan club, and going bowling with the bishop's daughter, and saving up for a Carpenters concert, but none of that really scratched the surface. I knew we'd both worked hard to create a safe surface, but I wanted to go below, where it wasn't safe.

"The problem was I could never make myself steal anything."

I was surprised how disappointed I felt to realize we were never going to do any deep pissing.

***

Two days later, though, we were back at the same market. I wanted to buy another postcard to send my mom. I found a great one of a small girl crying as a vendor threw a live eel into some boiling water. Another postcard I wanted to keep for myself—two women at night around a campfire on a desolate street corner next to a sign proclaiming "Puttane vere."

"Guarda," I said, pointing.

"You want some music?" Elder Grant asked as he surveyed the stand I'd indicated. "We can only play MoTab in the apartment."

Earlier on my mission, we'd also been able to listen to Mormon musicals like *My Turn on Earth* and *Saturday's Warrior*. One elder had requested permission to play classical music on his headphones while studying, which the mission president had granted. Then a sister had asked about playing generic "Christian" music, and the president had grudgingly consented to that as well.

Then another sister got caught listening to John Denver, and the mission president banned everything except the Mormon Tabernacle Choir.

"We can't watch TV when we visit the members," I said. "We can't go to a movie. We can't read newspapers. We can't have radios. We can't go to the beach because women here go topless sometimes. We can't visit Pompeii because it has sexual artwork." I looked off toward Vesuvius. "I want to listen to some Italian music."

I walked up to the stand and started browsing through the cassette tapes. Here was one by Fiordaliso, another by Zucchero, still another by Stefano Sani. There was a group called Pooh, another group named Ricchi e Poveri, and a rather pretty woman with the name of Elisabetta Viviani. I wondered if this was the best of Pop or if the vendor was getting rid of the crap no one wanted.

I picked up a tape featuring Claudio Baglioni.

"He needs a haircut," Elder Grant said.

I had no way to determine which of these artists, if any, I might like.

"Quanto?" I asked a heavyset man around thirty, flicking the ashes of his cigarette onto the cassettes nearest him.

"Tre mila."

Three thousand lire. It would mean skipping gelato or pizza bianca tonight while we were tracting. Disappointing because I really enjoyed watching Elder Grant lick off the vanilla ice cream that dripped onto his hand. "Va bene." I handed the man two of my thousand lire notes featuring La Scala and two more five hundred lire bills displaying Mercury's face. I couldn't imagine fifty cent notes ever being printed in the U.S. Or the equivalent of five lire coins worth less than half a cent. Sometimes, when stores ran out of change, they paid us in candy.

"You going to buy anything?" I asked my companion.

"I don't want to break any more rules than I have to."

"One day," I said, putting my hand on his wrist, "we'll be back in the States and want something to help us summon back our time here."

The reminder of our inevitable separation dampened the excitement of sneaking in a little culture. I recalled passing a bookstore a few days earlier and seeing a copy of *Guerre Stellari* in the window. How fun it would be to read about Luke Skywalker in Italian. The store had a copy of Bob Shaw's *Passeggiata Notturna* as well.

What I really needed, though, was a book written by an Italian author, maybe even someone Napoletano.

Did anyone here write about two men loving each other?

Elder Grant reached for a cassette containing songs by someone named Riccardo Fogli. He handed a five thousand lire note to the vendor, who shook his head. "Exact change."

Elder Grant turned to me, and I pulled my wallet back out. "I have another thousand lire bill," I told him.

He looked back at the stony-faced vendor and nodded for me to hand him the bill. Elder Grant picked up a second music tape, this one featuring Loretta Goggi, and handed over his six thousand lire. The vendor waved us away so other pedestrians could take a look at his merchandise.

Elder Grant and I headed off with at least three hours of Italian pop music. Listening together on P-Day sounded lovely, but I didn't think I could wait that long. We stopped in a shop to buy some fresh batteries for Elder Grant's cassette recorder, and then we ducked into a bookstore near the Galleria. I bought a copy of *Il nome della rosa* by Umberto Eco. It looked a bit intimidating, but it seemed to be about monks secluded together, and I thought it might be the closest I could get to a book about us.

We caught a bus up the hill and walked slowly along Via Nicolardi. Sometimes, it was a relief to get back to the apartment. Other times, I wanted to stay away as long as possible.

It was Elder Grant's turn to wash dishes after lunch, so I stayed in the kitchen after the other elders returned to their rooms until we were all supposed to leave again at 3:30. I took the opportunity to start passing off Colloquio H, the commandments. We rarely got far enough with any investigators to teach an H, so we recited it from memory at least once a month to make sure we'd remember it if we were ever lucky enough to need it.

"I hate when Elder Hatch cooks fegato," Elder Grant grumbled, not even paying attention to my brilliant recital of concepts 1 and 2. Not a single error. "He knows Elder Murdock and I both hate liver. He does it just so he can eat more himself. It's not fair. We all put into the grocery fund."

"I think he's getting back at Elder Murdock for embarrassing him at church last Sunday. You're just a victim of friendly fire."

"And we don't have enough money to buy a treat tonight."

I'd been cutting back lately to try to make up for so many extravagances earlier in the month. "Maybe we can make a sign. 'Will preach gospel for food.'"

Elder Grant laughed. "We'd starve to death!"

"Maybe 'Will stop talking about religion for food'?" I asked.

Elder Grant raised an eyebrow.

"I'll spring for some taralli," I said. "They're not too expensive. I like the ones with fennel."

My companion looked around furtively before quickly pecking me on the lips. "Then I'd better get a kiss in now," he whispered and pecked me again. "I don't like finocchio."

"Anziano," I whispered back. "*We're* finocchi." I only just now realized we'd never used the word in that context before. "I'll get you one with poppy seeds instead."

Elder Grant put the last dish in the drainboard, and we started down the hall to our room. Once we'd closed the door, I tried to start on the next concept in H when suddenly Elder Grant took a deep breath.

"What?"

"Those cassettes," he said.

"Sí?"

"They were pirated."

"What makes you think so?"

"Three thousand lire for a tape?" he said. "Even without store overhead, that's too cheap." He pulled one of his new cassettes out of his top desk drawer and studied it a moment. "Look," he said. "The photo's blurry."

I'd noticed the same issue on mine but just attributed it to general Italian fudging on quality.

Like Italian shoes. And suits.

Porca vacca. This was pirated music.

But we listened to it, anyway. Elder Grant sneaked his cassette player out when we left for the evening. We were in the Bosco Reale by 4:00, so quiet it was like no longer being in Napoli. We found a spot amongst the trees that seemed even more secluded, and then Elder Grant pulled out his cassette player. I handed him Claudio Baglioni, and he inserted it into the device's opening. He clicked the lid shut, and we looked about nervously to see if anyone was watching.

"Better take off our nametags," Elder Grant suggested. We did so, and then he hit Play.

I wasn't sure what I thought at first. The music was a little like my first beignet. A few of the Single Adults had gone together to the French Quarter, and I'd suggested we try the Café du Monde. The others protested that even if we ordered milk, if anyone who knew us saw us there, they'd think we were ordering coffee. We had to avoid the appearance of evil. I'd gone in by myself, the others grumpily agreeing to wait for me on the levee. But when my order of beignets arrived, they were so foreign to my idea of doughnuts that the first two bites left me wondering if I should have made so much fuss to get in.

By the time I'd finished the third beignet, I was hooked.

When I rejoined my friends, though, I told them the experience wasn't all that exciting. I figured it was better to let them think they were right and I was wrong.

"Io me ne andrei" was pleasant enough. My companion and I kept staring at the cassette player, trying to make out as many words as we could. Claudio sang clearly, but music always distorted the language. "Questo piccolo grande amore" was even nicer. And by the time Claudio had finished singing, "Amore bello," I could see that Elder Grant was as captivated as I was. I covered a smile when I saw him fingering his short hair.

He set the cassette player on the ground with our other belongings as "E tu…" started to play. "May I?" he asked, holding out his hand.

I took it, and he pulled me close. We held onto each other and rocked slowly around in a circle, Elder Grant's cheek brushing against mine. Some combination of testosterone, adrenalin, and other hormones I'd never felt before flooded my veins.

This was why all the teens at church clamored for youth dances, why the Single Adults held a stake dance every single month. Dancing was *fun* when you were doing it with someone you liked.

I remembered a Boys State/Girls State dance in Baton Rouge, when I'd asked a girl onto the dance floor who other guys were ignoring. I realized I was no prize, but dances always struck me as gym class for the romantic. No one liked discovering neither team wanted you.

Elder Grant and I kept dancing until the tape stopped playing.

I was no longer a virgin. Not that I'd had sex, but I realized I'd just made love for the first time in my life.

Older, retired Mormons could serve missions together as couples.

"We need to find a music store," I said. "We'll buy legitimate copies of these tapes for us, and we'll give these to Sister Coticelli."

"Won't it be a sin to let *anyone* benefit from piracy?" Elder Grant asked.

I squeezed my companion's hand. "The sin was already committed when we handed over our money. We'll make amends at the music store. But there's no reason not to let some good come of our mistake."

"When life hands you a lemon?" Elder Grant asked.

I shook my head. "I think it's a sin not to take every opportunity available to make someone feel loved, whatever that opportunity is."

"And even if it requires its own sin." He nodded.

We didn't masturbate together when we came home that evening after our visit to the music store, a half hour with Elisabetta, and another few hours going door to door. Somehow, despite our physical hunger, and our longing for one another, we still felt sated.

Chapter Eight:
The Destruction of Pompeii

The street we were tracting in Vomero was quiet, with few people walking about. One palazzo had a rose vine in front with several white roses. Another building a few doors down had blooming hydrangeas. Vegetation of any kind outside of parks was rare. "Let's stop and smell the flowers," I said, not realizing until the words were out of my mouth how trite they sounded.

Sure enough, Elder Grant groaned. "Could you be a little more original, Elder Mortensen?" He was only gently mocking, though.

I stuck out my tongue and then did stop and sniff the blue flowers.

"Are you emotionally edified now?"

"Hmm," I said. "Non lo so." I looked at him with a frown.

"What?"

I tilted my head and kept staring.

"Cosa stai facendo?"

"Ah!" I said, snapping my fingers. I leaned forward and put my nose to Elder Grant's neck. He took a step back, but I moved with him.

"My new motto is going to be 'Stop and smell the neck.'"

My companion laughed. "Not sure that one will catch on."

I shrugged. "Then it'll just be our private motto." I tilted my head again, and Elder Grant leaned forward to put his nose against my skin.

"Yep," he said, standing straight again. "I confirm this motto. We'll give it a name and a blessing."

"The Sure Sign of the Neck?" I asked.

"'We will go down.'" Elder Grant kneeled before me on the sidewalk, and I gave a playful schiaffo to the side of his head.

The ground beneath the next palazzo we wanted to enter dropped off as we walked farther from the street. A pathway starting at street level became a short bridge before we reached the front door. Looking over the railing, I could see the ground eight or nine feet below.

Not a good place to be in an earthquake, I realized. But then, being inside wasn't any safer if the quake was large enough. The sisters in Pozzuolli, even farther from the epicenter of last year's quake than the local missionaries, had jumped off their bus when the streetlamps began waving back and forth in front of the driver like metronomes.

Elder Grant and I climbed four flights of stairs. The apartment building had an ascensore, but it cost ten lire. We didn't have such small change on us and didn't want to waste a 200 lire coin.

The door on the far right on the top floor had a hand-printed sign taped onto it, the lettering careful and clean. "Thieves have already taken everything valuable. Please don't break our new lock."

It was impossible to know how much truth there was to the message. We'd seen notices on other doors in the past claiming that the occupants were the "Brigatte Rosse" or "La sede centrale della Camorra" or even a "Laundry Depository for Infectious Disease Researchers."

Whatever it took to keep people out.

I knocked on the door. After a few moments, I rang the bell. We were just about to move to the next door when we heard rustling inside the apartment. Next came the sound of chains rattling and a lock being turned. A man swung the door open, a pistol pointed at us.

"Buona sera," I said with a smile. "We're representatives of The Church of Jesus Christ. How would you like to live in a world where you weren't afraid to open your door?"

"Madonna," the man grunted in disgust, shutting the door and relocking it.

"At least we planted a seed," Elder Grant said as we knocked on the next door.

"Stop and smell the seeds," I said but then shook my head. "I like our other motto better."

"Unless by seeds you mean…"

"Hmm. Can we have two official mottos?"

Down on the first floor, we talked to a thirty-year-old man for a few minutes about eternal marriage. Two buildings over, we spoke to another man about the blessing of modern revelation. In the following building, a woman asked if we knew her cousin in Chicago. When we claimed ignorance, the woman repeated her cousin's name again, enunciating slowly and loudly.

Neither of us had still ever been to Chicago.

"I wish there was a gelateria nearby," Elder Grant said after we left the building.

Or a bar where we could grab an acqua minerale. Even if our budget was already overstretched.

We climbed to the top floor of the next building and tracted our way down. The TV was blaring in one of the apartments on the second floor. I didn't want to intrude on anyone. A surprising number of people watched cartoons in the evening. I couldn't imagine such a thing ever happening in the U.S. I'd seen snippets of *Speed Racer* and *Jonny Quest* several times while we went door to door both here and back in Quartu.

Elder Grant rang the bell. After waiting almost a minute, he was about to try again when I shook my head and pointed to the next door. But before we could move, the door opened a few inches, revealing a woman's face. She was about thirty-five, with dark, wavy hair. And a black eye.

"Who is it?" a male voice shouted from deeper inside the apartment.

"Nessuno," the woman called back. But she didn't shut the door. "Can I help you?"

"Can we help *you*?" Elder Grant asked, rubbing his cheek with his index finger to point at his eye.

"Do you have a pamphlet you can leave?" she asked softly. I could barely hear her.

My companion quickly browsed through a small stack he always carried and pulled out Il Piano di Salvezza. He offered it toward the narrow opening. The woman started to reach for it.

When suddenly someone behind her jerked her back and slammed the door.

"You know I hate when you—" and then I couldn't make out any more, the words shouted quickly in a thick Napoletan accent. The man was almost certainly throwing in some dialect as well.

But the slap was clear enough to understand.

"Stop crying! You know I hate it when you cry!"

There was another slap. And another. Then the shouting stopped, though we could still hear soft sobbing.

I wasn't sure if spousal abuse was even illegal here. Or that the law was enforced if it was.

"Andiamo, Anziano," Elder Grant said, pulling me away.

We skipped the apartments in the rest of the building and stood quietly on the sidewalk out front for several minutes, not even looking at each other. Finally, Elder Grant cleared his throat. "Let's go," he said.

"Where?"

"I want a gelato."

***

"What do you think you're doing?" Elder Murdock demanded. "You can't leave the apartment in your P-Day clothes!" He'd been reprimanded publicly at our last zone conference for being too lenient. It was *his* job, President Alsop pointed out, to make sure the elders under his command were obedient enough to draw down the power of heaven.

"But it's P-Day," I pointed out.

"Jeans and casual shirts are for lounging around in the apartment. Or *cleaning*." He tapped his right foot. "Have you finished your chores?"

This week, the chore chart had assigned me to mop the kitchen and hallway. Elder Grant was to be cook for the following week. "Elder Mortensen's finished all of his," my companion said, "and I'll pick up groceries on our way back."

"Just where do you plan to go dressed like that?"

This was the tricky part, of course. After our visit with Antonio and Stefano a couple of weeks ago, I couldn't get the idea of going to Pompeii out of my mind. At orientation in the mission home my first day in Italy, I'd been disappointed to discover Pompeii and Herculaneum were off limits to missionaries because of the artwork we might see among the ruins. Missionaries in New Orleans likewise hadn't been allowed in the French Quarter. But regular members of the Church could see a female mannequin's legs swinging out of a stripper bar on Bourbon Street without complete moral collapse. So I found the mission rule arbitrary. We saw scantily clad women downtown every day. We passed a group of prostitutes every time we caught the bus in front of the Ospedale Cardarelli.

"You're not here to sightsee," President Alsop had told us. "You're here to preach the gospel." It was the same answer he gave for everything. We weren't here to learn Roman or Greek or Spanish history. We weren't here to learn about the Catholic Church. We weren't here to learn about World War II, or opera, or Sophia Loren.

"We're going to the Museo di Capodimonte," I said, "and then take a long, relaxing walk through the park." I glanced at Elder Grant. "We might even lie on the grass in the sun. That's why we don't want to wear our suits."

"Oh! I want to go!" It was Elder Booth, who'd replaced Elder Crandall in the last transfers.

"Well, *I* don't want to," said Elder Hatch. "We only get one day off a week, and I'm not wasting it at a museum."

"That's okay," Elder Booth replied. "You can stay with the zone leaders, and I'll tag along with these guys. We'll be a threesome for the day."

For a brief moment, I envisioned exactly that, but since all Elder Booth ever talked about was his girlfriend back in St. George, I didn't think he was gay enough to masturbate with us.

"*I* want to play soccer with some of the guys from the branch," Elder Hatch said. "So you have to stay with me."

"Aw, pick."

"Maybe another time, Elder," my companion said.

"I haven't given you my permission yet," Elder Murdock reminded us.

Suddenly, everyone stopped talking. And moving. Just eyes darting about.

"I...don't remember asking for permission," I replied.

Elder Booth gasped.

"Come on, Elder Mortensen," Elder Grant said, opening the door. "Let's get on with our P-Day."

***

"He's going to ask President Alsop to separate us," Elder Grant warned as we waited for the bus to Pompeii.

"Lo so." But what, really, could I do about it? If we lived 100% by the rules, being together would be virtually meaningless, anyway. Our only hope was to live the best we could for as long as we could. Enduring to the end had taken on a new meaning.

At almost every zone conference, the mission president reminded us that our mission was the trial run for our life. If we were lazy and unproductive here, we'd be lazy in our careers back home. If we went home early, we'd be quitters and losers the rest of our lives. If we were unfaithful here, at a time when the Lord was bestowing blessings upon us daily, we'd never have the faith later to heal our sick children. And if we broke rules here, we'd set patterns that would prevent us from living the commandments back home and end up in one of the lower kingdoms without our families on Judgment Day.

Thank God it would be at least three more months before another zone conference, no matter which zone I was in. The president had just finished making the rounds yet again.

"We'll be separated all too soon as it is, Elder Mortensen," my companion went on. "We've already made it through three transfers. We won't make it past a fourth."

He looked away. "Especially if you make Elder Murdock mad."

"We'll pick up a couple of ciambelle for him on the way back."

"Oh, Anziano." Elder Grant rubbed his sternum. "You're going through so much money."

My father had noted the same thing in a recent letter, the first time he'd written the mandatory weekly epistle instead of my mother. I'd written back that we had a poor elder serving in our district and that all the rest of us who shared the apartment were helping to cover his expenses. I assured my father that either he or I would undoubtedly be transferred soon, and my expenses would then return to normal.

The only hope I had of getting back in control of my mission allowance was to be separated from Elder Grant.

But what hope was there to be had in such an unhappy future? I promised my father I'd pay him back when I graduated college, that I wanted him to keep a record of every penny, and to charge a reasonable interest rate.

In my own head, I tried to keep any vision of the future hazy, afraid to look too closely.

I pointed down the street. "L'autobus."

Such an easy word.

After we boarded, standing near the middle of the bus heading south, I studied the other passengers around us.

Most of the tourists were couples or families. That was the way the world worked. My companion and I were living in a bubble. If we were really married, working normal jobs, living ordinary lives, would we bicker over money? Over what TV show to watch? Over how to furnish our home?

How wonderful it must be, I thought, to have the chance to bicker.

I thought back to the incident with Elder Murdock.

No, bickering really wasn't much fun.

"I'm sorry, Anziano," I said. "I'll try to be more careful."

But my resolve didn't last long. Once we stepped off the bus, I tried to hold Elder Grant's hand.

"Anziano!" he hissed. "We're not in an alley somewhere!"

"We're in P-Day clothes," I reminded him. "We took off our nametags as soon as we left the apartment. And no other missionaries will be here."

I could feel the sweat on my companion's palm, but he still managed to grip my hand back tightly. That alone was worth risking Elder Murdock's wrath. It almost didn't matter where we were today. I expected the only enduring memory I'd have of the place was holding Elder Grant's hand. As we walked slowly about the ruins, though, I realized I didn't know very much about what had taken place here. I'd always assumed the city was buried intact. I hadn't realized both Pompeii and Herculaneum were knocked down first. Almost none of the ruins was over a few feet high except where broken pieces had been fitted back together. Still, there was enough to give me an idea of what the area must have looked like in its heyday.

Courtyards, baths, public toilets. Beautiful columns. Amphoras originally filled with wine. And the artwork— the main reason we'd worked up the courage to come in the first place.

Mosaics showing a dog, some ducks, an octopus, birds drinking from a bird bath, a cat. Frescoes portraying a robed woman with a book in her hand, of gladiators fighting, of a centaur bowing before a man. Other frescoes revealed a woman playing a lyre, a family being served dinner by their servants or perhaps their slaves. In what must have been a bordello, other frescoes detailed various sex acts.

All of these in the last group, it seemed, showed men and women interacting. There was one depicting several men lounging together and eating something. Grapes? But it wasn't clear the men were about to engage in sex.

"Good grief!" I muttered aloud.

"Cosa?"

"I've been *hoping* to be seduced by the Dark Side."

"Boh."

"You know, the Force and all that."

"You don't find it exciting at all to see those frescoes?"

I stopped in front of another one, a woman sitting down on a man's penis. It was exactly what I wanted to do. And yet...

"It might be fun to wear togas sometime instead of garments," I said, "when we masturbate."

"Shh!" Elder Grant pointed to a young girl, probably nine or ten, who was staring at the fresco along with her parents. The girl was red-headed and probably didn't understand Italian, but he had a point.

"Let's go to the next building," I said.

And that was when we finally saw what we'd come for. A man against a light blue background stood facing us, his uncircumcised penis impossibly large, maybe twelve or thirteen inches long. Someone passing nearby noted it was the god Priapus. I'd never heard of him.

Peccato. That would be a god easy to get behind. Or in front of. Well, maybe not *easy*...

One room over, though, Elder Grant and I shouted at the same time.

"O Dio!"

"Porca la Madonna!"

A man walking across a yellow background had an erect cock as long and as big around as one of his legs. A thirty or forty pound dick.

I hoped there were postcards at the gift shop.

Elder Grant and I stood staring for several minutes. His grasp on my hand slowly loosened, and after a few more minutes, he turned to me. "Heavenly Father didn't make us companions in Caserta or Rome or Cagliari," he said. "He sent us both to this mission, but he put us together in Napoli. That can't be an accident."

"You'll finish your mission several months ahead of me," I reminded him.

"I'll go to prepare a place for you." He smiled, knowing I'd understand the reference.

I wanted to kiss him, but even in a place like this, I didn't dare.

We continued our tour of the ruins and finally came upon the remains of Romans who'd been killed. They weren't the actual bodies of the victims, of course. Most of those had disintegrated over time. But they'd left hollows in the hardened ash. Scientists had filled the holes with plaster, and we got to see the last moments for the inhabitants of Pompeii.

It was hard to tell the men from the women but easy to distinguish the children from the adults. Bodies of both were sprawled face down, or curled in a fetal position, some covering their faces with their hands. Arms and legs were frozen in place as victims flailed about, apparently buried in ash while still struggling. A dog curled violently as if trying to bite through the rope tethering him to his death.

Elder Grant stared in horror but then slowly turned to me. "Why are you crying?" he asked.

"What if," I began, "what if we aren't sent to Outer Darkness together? What if there are different degrees, like there are in heaven?"

I didn't buy any postcards on our way back to the bus. We did stop at a pasticceria in the city so I could buy two doughnuts for Elder Murdock. And Elder Grant, with a look of heroic determination, plopped down a few hundred lire to buy a cannolo for me.

Chapter Nine:
Sailors and Whores

"Mom's package!" I said when Elder Murdock brought the mail in from the lobby.

"If it's food," Elder Murdock returned, "you have to share it with the whole district."

"It's postcards."

Elder Murdock frowned. "American postcards?"

"They're for Sorella Coticelli." I didn't explain further.

I'd mailed my mom over a month ago, asking her to go through the postcards I'd saved from our family vacations—trips to the Grand Canyon, Yellowstone, the Petrified Forest, Yosemite, Sequoia National Park, Joshua Tree, and, of course, Salt Lake City.

"You're just going to hand her a bunch of old postcards?" Elder Murdock asked, still standing in our doorway.

I looked up at him. "We're going to write happy thoughts on the back of each one so she can always feel encouraged when she looks at them."

"Happy thoughts? Shouldn't you at least quote scripture verses, Elder Mortensen?" He looked so unhappy I wondered if I should set one card aside for him.

But what message would I put on it?

"We're going to write happy thoughts," I repeated. I handed several cards to Elder Grant, who placed them face down on his desk and picked up a pen. I'd bought him one with purple ink and another for me with green, just for Elisabetta's postcards.

"You're not doing it *now*, are you?" Elder Murdock asked in disbelief. "Lunch hour is almost over, and that sounds like a P-Day activity."

I looked back up at him without replying.

"Even on P-Day, it's a waste of time," Elder Murdock continued. "That woman's a *simpatizzante eterna*. She's never going to get baptized." He bit his lip, glancing at his watch.

Elder Grant, without looking up from his desk, said, "I'm the senior, and we're doing *this* today. It's missionary work."

The conviction with which he said it triggered a surge of hormones from my testicles and adrenal glands. I was afraid Elder Murdock might see my dick twitch.

He stood silently for a long moment. Then he slapped the door jamb. "You guys get weirder every day. If you're not careful, I'll have to report you." He moved off down the hall. I crossed over to shut the door and then placed the first few cards on my desk blank side up, trying to compose happy thoughts that wouldn't sound too generic but would instead help Elisabetta know we were thinking of her and no one else when we wrote them.

***

The *USS Nimitz* was in town, and we could see sailors everywhere. The Navy base just north of the city was only one of several factors in the substantial number of blond-haired Napoletani we saw every day. But it seemed that most of the sailors roaming about did their roaming in pairs. Were they ordered to stick together, like missionaries, or…?

"I heard there are more gays in the Navy than in other branches of the military," I said, stopping to watch two young men about our age looking at a long row of stands selling tomatoes and zucchini and women's panties.

"Those two guys kind of look like us," Elder Grant noted. "The cute one has dark hair like you, and the other has hair almost like mine."

I laughed. "The same length, too." I nudged my companion in the side. "Interesting observation, though."

"Che intendi?"

"I think the sailor with hair like *yours* is the cute one."

It was Elder Grant's turn to laugh now. "I wonder…" he began.

"Yes?"

"If they're gay, we could maybe ask them what it's like."

"They might not be able to say anything," I pointed out. "They're probably afraid they'll get kicked out of the military."

"But maybe…"

Something about the men was magnetic. And if being with Elder Grant had taught me anything, it was that sometimes, we needed to be bold. "Let's go chat for a few minutes," I suggested. We walked over with a wave, and I asked the sailors, in English, "How's life in America these days?"

"We wouldn't know," the dark-haired man replied.

We introduced ourselves, and the two men told us their names were Seaman Nylander and Seaman Tate.

"Is this your first time in Italy?" Elder Grant asked.

"First time in Naples," Seaman Nylander, the lighter-haired man, told us. The two men exchanged glances. "Can you guys show us around?"

It was the question I'd been hoping for, yet now I realized how stupid a thing it was to want. What did either of us know about gay life in Napoli? Or about anything else these guys might be interested in? The bars Elder Grant and I frequented sold hazelnut and vanilla sodas. They had pinball machines. Maybe a freezer of chocolate-covered ice cream cones.

And if these guys were straight, which was far more likely...

"Anything in particular you want to see?" I asked.

Seaman Tate chuckled. "We're at sea all the time. We want to meet some women." He chuckled again. "You Mormons always have extra women lying around, don't you?" He put an unnatural emphasis on the word "lying."

Maybe this wasn't such a great idea. "We don't really—" I began.

"How do you guys cope all that time at sea without women?" Elder Grant interrupted. I wondered if he was consciously adapting the question I'd asked on the ferry from Cagliari. At least we knew these guys understood the words.

The two sailors exchanged glances again. Seaman Nylander swaggered half a step closer. "There are usually a couple of guys on every ship who like to suck dick," he said. "And there's always that one..." He slapped his shipmate heartily on the back. "...who will take it up the ass."

"You know I'm straight!" Seaman Tate protested.

"Sure, sure."

"It's just that I don't mind...I mean, I'm okay with taking one for the team."

"Never volunteer for anything," his buddy reminded him.

Oh my heck. Had they really just confessed all that right in front of us? I noticed a slight lump in the front of Elder Grant's loose dress pants. But what now? Did we simply start asking questions? I didn't even know what to ask. And if all they did was regular oral and anal sex, the possibility struck me that we might know more than they did.

That couldn't be good.

"I'm not sure where to find pick-up bars," I said.

"We're looking for whores," Seaman Nylander clarified.

I thought about the Ospedale Cardarelli, but those women were only at their post in the evening. "We can head into the centro storico," I said. "It's a pretty poor area of town, so maybe we'll run across something." I looked at Elder Grant, who was frowning. "You guys probably know what to look for better than we do."

"Oh, I don't know," Seaman Nylander said, chucking me playfully under the chin. "I can tell you guys know more than you're letting on." He looked at Elder Grant and then back again at me. "Right?"

"Um…"

Nylander laughed. "I'm just being a prick," he said. "Come on. Show us around. You tell us what little you know, and we'll tell you *all* the stuff we know."

The scariest part of town I'd ever seen was a stop along the funicolare. Elder Grant and I had stepped out one evening, too early to head back to the apartment but already dark, and I instantly sensed that the poverty here was of a different quality than I'd witnessed elsewhere. It was like accidentally getting off the bus on Julia Street back in New Orleans, or Melpomene, like finding yourself unexpectedly right in the middle of the Desire projects. There was no shortage of dangerous spots in New Orleans, but this was the first time I'd ever been frightened in Italy. I had just been about to suggest we get back on the funicolare when an old woman came up to us, wagging her finger. "These streets no good for you!" she croaked in English. "These streets no good!"

I had known with every fiber of my being that she was telling the truth. I thanked her, grabbed my companion's arm, and hurried away with him as quickly as I could.

But in the daytime, perhaps it wouldn't be so bad, and maybe it was exactly what these guys were after. I motioned for them to follow, and we all headed deeper into the ghetto. The sailors joked over the next several minutes about every busty woman who passed by. I'd never realized how many busty women there were. Denied appropriate outlets for their sexual energy for quite some time, the sailors were verbally lusting even after women in their forties.

"And that woman," Seaman Nylander said, indicating a tall brunette with striking legs, "is a man."

"Huh?" said Elder Grant.

"See the Adam's apple?" Nylander went on.

"Ah."

"Yeah, you go off with a few of those women, you soon learn what to look for." He pulled out his wallet and retrieved a photograph. "Simona hardly has any Adam's apple at all."

"Simona?" Elder Grant asked.

"She's his girl in Sigonella," Seaman Tate said. The two sailors laughed.

Oh my heck.

It was hard to hear much of the rest of the conversation over the next several minutes, my own thoughts bouncing about so loudly inside my head. Could a man be straight and still want sex with another man? Could he be straight and still like a woman with a penis?

What if this also meant I could be gay and still like sex with a woman? Perhaps I could get married in the temple, after all. I wondered if there was a term for having one wife *and* one husband. Monoandrygamy?

I wanted Elder Grant.

Suddenly, Seaman Nylander grabbed me by my tie and shoved me against a rough stone wall. Elder Grant's back struck the wall beside me as he was slammed against some vulgar graffiti by Seaman Tate. Were they about to kiss us? While my companion and I had tried many things, neither of us was into brutish behavior. Sweaty balls were one thing but—

A knee crashed into my groin. A punch to my stomach was followed by a slap to my face, and another blow to my chin. I heard my nametag clatter onto the huge black stones of the street.

I didn't fight back. I didn't know how. My Young Men's teacher had brought a judo instructor to class one Wednesday evening, but I simply wasn't interested.

I curled up on the enormous blocks, thinking back to the body of a child I'd seen in Pompeii. I wanted to look for my companion, was afraid to look for him. I was vaguely aware of people passing us on the street, keeping their eyes averted. It was hard to focus, my head moving along with the rest of my body with every kick. A few moments later, my head lying on a rough black stone, I watched feet calmly walking by. No one was even hurrying to get away.

"God, I hate you fucking faggots." With a last kick to my ribs, Nylander stalked off, followed by his friend.

I was afraid to move, afraid it would hurt even more, afraid it might entice them to come back. I felt more intensely aware of my body than I ever had, more keenly even than the first night Elder Grant and I had masturbated together.

I wondered if any blood vessels inside my brain were torn where I'd been kicked in the head. I tried to sense if my spleen had ruptured. What if I had blood in my intestines that dripped out my rectum? If a doctor examined me, he might be able to tell what Elder Grant and I had been doing.

Suddenly, I realized the opportunity we'd just lost.

It wasn't fair.

Why couldn't Heavenly Father simply have let them kill us? Even if he still needed to damn us on Judgment Day, at least our families would never have to learn who we really were during their mortal lives, which was always going to be a danger as long as we breathed.

It was so…so mean.

"Anziano." I felt Elder Grant's hands fumbling for me. "Stai bene? Stai bene?"

I pulled myself painfully to a sitting position, feeling something stretch inside my abdomen that wasn't supposed to stretch. My left knee hurt something awful, and the fingernail on my right index finger had somehow been ripped off. Mannaggia, that stung. It was the finger I used most to enter my companion.

My scoutmaster had been a big fan of making sure the punishment always fit the crime. He'd tied my hands to a tree for an hour the day I failed to successfully demonstrate the knots he'd assigned.

"Poverino mio," Elder Grant murmured, wincing and putting his finger to his lips. The lower one was cracked, blood covering half of his formerly white shirt. His right cheek was cut, his pants filthy. His left forearm already had a deep bruise.

I dreaded the thought of buying a new suit. Perhaps I could get by with just the one I had left.

I might not even need that if we got sent home.

Elder Grant and I helped each other to our feet. He rubbed something off my face.

A middle-aged woman came over and touched my arm gingerly. "You boys better leave. People around here know if you're hurt, you're weak." She pointed in the direction we should go, and even realizing she might be leading us to the callused fists or pickpocketing fingers of her waiting husband and his pals, we stumbled off the way she'd suggested.

The worst part, the absolute worst part, of the entire experience was the other elders instantly assuming we'd been assaulted because we were missionaries. And how neither Elder Grant nor I had the courage to tell them anything remotely resembling the truth. We didn't even muster the decency to say we'd been mugged. We accepted everyone's admiration and praise and awe, knowing it was a more despicable sin than anything we'd ever done together in the dark.

***

Sorrento was outside our area, even outside our mission, twenty kilometers south of Castellammare di Stabia. I'd long been intrigued when I realized how close it was to Napoli, since I'd passed through Sorrento, Louisiana many times in my childhood. When Elder Murdock mentioned he and his companion had gone to commission a piece of wooden inlay artwork depicting the Salt Lake temple for his mother, I decided to follow their example. I wasn't quite sure what wooden inlay artwork was, but after breaking through the invisible wall keeping us out of Pompeii, I wanted to venture just a little farther from my pen.

I remembered the dog caught in its death throes trying to bite through its restraint.

The previous week, Elder Grant and I boarded a train heading south on the Circumvesuviana line, wandered about the seaside town, and discovered several shops that specialized in marquetry. Intursio di legno. I had to look it up. As zone leaders, Elders Murdock and Rasmussen could flout the rules that we couldn't. For peasants like us, leaving the mission was a transgression serious enough to trigger being sent home in disgrace.

My companion and I made our way back to the shop this morning just before noon and picked up our wooden inlay artwork, a portrait of me for Elder Grant and a portrait of Elder Grant for me. Each one, about the size of a piece of typing paper and as thick as maybe two pieces of cardboard, consisted of multiple, specially cut fragments pieced together to recreate a sepia-type image from photographs taken before our recent pummeling. Kind of like Paint-by-Number, only with wood. Portraits were far more intricate achievements than reproducing an image of the temple, so even though we hired the most reasonable artisan we could find, they still cost a whopping twenty-seven mila lire each.

We'd discovered, though, when talking with medical staff at the hospital in Vomero, that we could make a little extra money selling blood plasma. Of course, a few mila lire twice a week wasn't going to get us far. I'd heard about sperm donation back in New Orleans but didn't bother asking about it here, since it would likely require that my companion and I not masturbate for two or three days before each deposit.

"I love it," Elder Grant said, hugging the portrait of my face to his chest.

Every time I visited my father at work, I smiled to see he kept a photo of Mom on his desk.

I wondered what kind of job I could find that would allow me to keep a portrait of Elder Grant on mine.

I slid my companion's face between the pages of my flip charts, and he slid his portrait of me in between his scriptures.

Walking slowly back to the train station, we stopped for a gelato. Nocciola for me and fragole for him. Why not? My father was about to disown me as it was over my continually escalating expenses. What difference did a few thousand more lire make? I didn't dare think what might happen if he confronted President Alsop about the pretense I'd given him.

What if I just stopped being a missionary altogether, I thought, and found a job instead? I knew how to be a portiere. I'd talked with enough of them, after all, before they kicked us out of their buildings. I could be a postino. I could work in a formaggeria. I could learn how to bake bread, or work in an alimentari.

"Anziano Grant." I pointed to a movie poster glued to the wall beside us. Ten or eleven identical posters were plastered next to one another advertising a film called *Ciao marziano*.

"Beh?"

"Let's go see a movie." I realized with a smile I'd delivered the line the same way Mary Badham had said, "Let's kill Uncle first!" in a cheesy William Castle flick.

"Elder Mortensen! Movies are against the rules!"

I thought of suggesting we sit in the back row and neck, but I wasn't really after physical intimacy. "I want to be normal."

My companion stood facing the poster for a long moment and then nodded.

I paid our admission, and we sat in the middle of the theater to get a good view of the screen. We didn't kiss when the lights dimmed, but we did hold hands. The film was about a Martian sent to Rome to study human behavior. A comedy.

I felt like Will Robinson again.

One of my Sunday School teachers had warned us each week of the danger in smoking even one cigarette, drinking even one beer, taking even one hit of LSD. "Once you've seen Paris," he said, "you can never go back to the farm."

I wasn't sure I could go back to Mars.

We sat through the very end of the closing credits and then walked out of the darkened theater. "Let's run away, Anziano." Before Elder Grant could respond, I marched over to the girl at the ticket counter to ask if they were hiring. She shook her head and then took a slow drag from her cigarette.

We popped into five more stores on our way back to the station. No one was hiring.

Just how did an American go about finding a job in another country, I wondered. Perhaps I could do something at the embassy in Rome. I might be able to apply for a scholarship to one of the universities in Padova or Bologna. Surely, I could—

Elder Grant grabbed my shoulders. "Anziano, Jonah couldn't run away, and we can't, either." He pulled me close, and we hugged for several minutes, long enough to hear Diana Ross's "Upside Down" streaming out an open window from someone's apartment, followed by "Un'altra vita, un altro amore," sung by a man with a mesmerizing voice.

Being swallowed by a whale was no big deal, I thought. It was nothing compared to being swallowed whole by God.

Chapter Ten:
Lights On

"So the First Nephite shoots onto the face of the Second Nephite," I whispered, "and then the Third Nephite licks it off."

Elder Grant moaned softly, his fingers lightly caressing my cheek. "How about this?" he asked. "The Second Nephite shoots into the mouth of the Third Nephite, and then the Third Nephite Lamanite-kisses the First Nephite and passes it all to him."

"Mi piace," I whispered.

"And then the First Nephite spits it into the Third Nephite's crack, and the Second Nephite licks back up his own cum."

I wondered if it would be possible to keep coming up with new ideas if we were sealed together for eternity. After all, some of the variations were pretty minor. Would physical intimacy get boring after two thousand years? After twelve thousand? A million? The challenge didn't feel daunting but exciting to contemplate. "I've got another," I whispered, a little too loudly.

"Shh."

"The First Nephite shoots onto the Second Nephite's asshole," I whispered more softly, "and then the Third Nephite uses that as lube so he can slide into the Second Nephite's ass. The First Nephite gets down and licks the balls of the Second Nephite while he's getting fucked." I took a deep breath, knowing four-letter words were every bit as sinful as masturbation, even if we were saying them in Italian. "And when the Third Nephite cums inside the Second Nephite, the First Nephite stays there and licks the cum when he squeezes it out of his ass for him."

"So the First and the Third Nephite's cum is all mixed together." I could feel Elder Grant's penis tenting out from his garments and just barely brushing against me.

"Yes," I said, "and with it still in his mouth, he sucks off the Second Nephite and gets *all* their cum in his mouth." I leaned forward in the darkness until my companion's breath on my face told me I was close. Then I reached out and pulled his face toward mine. Elder Grant's tongue dove deep into my mouth. The act was familiar and comforting and yet somehow always new, a revelation. The taste of his mint toothpaste was pleasant but not as soothing as a mouthful of Nephite cum would have been.

But when it would come time to kiss later before finally going to bed…

As many different things as we tried together, it never felt like we'd tried enough. I wanted his tongue in my mouth *and* my ass simultaneously. I wanted his dick in both openings at the same time. I wanted a finger, or two fingers, or three in my ass along with his dick and his tongue.

"Kneel over the bed," Elder Grant whispered a bit too loudly. I'd never been able to project. I ended up as Elder Green in our stake's production of *Saturday's Warrior* when I felt quite sure I could have handled the role of Todd.

I thought I understood now the funny look the director had given me when I asked to audition for the romantic lead.

I reached out to put my finger over my companion's lips. He licked it, and then I turned to face the wall, hoping he'd figure out something new to try but not wanting to pass on a chance to repeat the wonderful things we'd already done on other evenings.

Elder Grant pried open the slit in the seat of my garments. I heard a squirt and soon felt conditioner on my asshole. Would he use a finger again? A zucchini?

Would he finally use…?

No, we couldn't let ourselves do that.

But what if he pulled out before cumming?

I felt one finger slide inside me, going deep to the hilt. Elder Grant pulled it out to my sphincter, toyed with the muscle a moment, and then slid a second finger in, pushing both all the way inside.

"Ahh."

My companion pulled his fingers out to the edge of my asshole again and now carefully inserted a third.

"Stai bene?"

"Sí!" Come no? Magari potesse…

My companion then pushed all three fingers in as far as they would go. He pressed them against the side of my rectum. He turned his hand about and pressed against the other side. He pulled his fingers back an inch and pushed them back in, pressing the butt of his hand hard against my asshole.

Then he pulled out to my sphincter again and, though I didn't think it possible, gently inserted a fourth finger.

"Oh my god," I said, in English, with a short gasp.

Elder Grant paused, whether from my gasp or because I'd taken the Lord's name in vain, I didn't know, but then slowly pushed all four fingers deep inside me.

Was he going to do more? Could he? And could I take it if he did?

"Per favore," I whispered. "Bisogno ho di te." I hadn't meant to quote "I Need Thee Every Hour."

Elder Grant pulled his four fingers out and toyed another moment with my sphincter, teasing me by adding his thumb to the rest, but only just barely edging past the gate. I thought I was going to shoot before he finished putting all five fingers in.

His thumb slid in deeper next to his other fingers. I felt the knuckle move through, and I moaned.

I reached through the slit in front of my garments and wiped a heavy drop of pre-cum off the tip of my penis. Some had already been absorbed by the fabric, but I still got a good taste. Sweet.

My companion pushed in as deep as he could, but the rest of his hand where all the knuckles converged at the base was just too huge to allow further penetration.

"Imagine," Elder Grant whispered, "the First Nephite and Second Nephite both putting their dicks inside the Third Nephite at the same time."

I felt my sphincter tighten, but Elder Grant pushed forward gently to loosen me up again. He kept pushing, always calmly but insistently. My ass wouldn't give anymore, but he didn't stop the mild pressure. I felt his hand move a few millimeters deeper. And another millimeter. And another.

It was all I could do not to shove my ass backwards onto his hand, the way *The Blob* had jumped onto the old man's hand after he extracted the creature from the meteorite. But even fleeting images of Steve McQueen couldn't keep me from focusing on my companion. Elder Grant was using his right hand, and I imagined the act being turned into a new ordinance. Instead of raising one's arm to the square...

The bedroom door opened and the light snapped on, blinding us as much as the darkness had.

"Che fate!?" Elder Murdock demanded.

Elder Grant withdrew his hand immediately, making me gasp.

I hoped gasps didn't automatically imply guilt.

"Elder Mortensen has terrible hemorrhoids," Elder Grant said without a second's hesitation. I wondered if he'd rehearsed this scenario for emergencies. "I asked if I could apply the ointment," he continued, "as a way of humbling myself." I squinted against the glare to see what was happening, still leaning over the bed.

"Hemorrhoids?" Elder Murdock's tone sounded more bewildered than disbelieving.

"They're really big." Elder Grant pried open my back slit more widely. "You want to take a look?"

"Ugh."

"I know. That's why I insisted we turn out the light. I'm not that humble *yet*." He made a sound halfway between a sigh and a whistle. "It wouldn't hurt you to humble yourself a little more, too, you know." He held out the small bottle of conditioner, which looked nothing like a tube of ointment. I could only hope Elder Murdock was too stunned to pay close attention. "You want to apply some?" He paused. "A little bit?"

"Cretini," Elder Murdock mumbled. "You're flippin' nuts." He shook his head.

"Maybe I'll use this story in a General Conference talk one day when I'm 70." Elder Grant gave a little smile.

"Elder Mortensen," Elder Murdock said wearily, "put the medicine on your own damn butt. And for Pete's sake, guys, get to sleep. It's after Lights Out, and we can all hear you rustling around. É fastidioso."

Elder Murdock turned off the light and closed the door on his way out. Had he not noticed the large tent in the front of Elder Grant's garments? Or mine? Maybe, I hoped, he was so distracted by Elder Grant touching my ass that he missed everything else.

But then, I remembered the Cartwright family in my ward back home. The second oldest child, a year younger than me, looked quite different from the other kids in the family, so much swarthier and with exceptionally curly hair. I'd graduated from Seminary and joined the Single Adults group before I realized he was black.

I sent up a prayer of thanks as Elder Murdock's footsteps faded away. Even if masturbation was only a minor sin, though, surely Heavenly Father wouldn't really have *helped* me. Would he?

"We better call it quits for tonight," Elder Grant whispered.

"Not yet," I said. "Put three fingers back inside me while I beat off."

"I'm not up to eating your cum tonight."

"Capisco," I said, trying to hide my disappointment, "but I'm going to drink a mouthful of cum, even if it's mine." Everything we did involved fantasizing that we were doing something more anyway.

I heard Elder Grant apply new conditioner to his fingers, and soon he was back inside my ass. I pulled out my dick and shot into my hand within another thirty seconds. Elder Grant withdrew, and I turned to face him in the darkness, pulling him toward me until our crotches pressed against each other.

I slurped the cum off my hand but couldn't bear to swallow just yet. I put both arms around my companion and held him close.

My own cum in my mouth, and both of us still encased in our sacred garments, I felt more distant from my companion than ever.

If only…

Elder Grant's mushroomy penis was still hard against me.

I didn't want to swallow and permit the evening to end.

Lips pressed against mine without warning, and Elder Grant's tongue dug hungrily into my mouth. His tongue and saliva changed the taste of my cum, and neither of us wanted to swallow and have to retire to our cots. We passed my semen back and forth until it somehow dissipated into nothingness.

We pulled apart, still holding hands.

I felt the way I had when Mary Steenburgen jumped into the Time Machine and sat on Malcolm McDowell's lap after he killed Jack the Ripper. Somehow, no matter what upheaval lay ahead, everything was going to be okay.

Unless we were being just as willfully blind as Elder Murdock.

"Sogni d'oro," I whispered.

"No," said Elder Grant. "Sogni bianchi." He kissed my forehead.

I climbed into my bed with a smile, choosing to be happy again despite everything, and thanked Heavenly Father once more.

***

I awoke sometime in the middle of the night, the room still pitch black because of the lowered serranda. I listened to Elder Grant's steady breathing while I stared up into the darkness, my sphincter tingling a little from its earlier abuse. Whatever endorphins had flooded my bloodstream earlier all seemed to have broken down or been absorbed.

We really were getting perverted, I realized. What kind of freaks smelled armpits, or pissed onto their companion's dick when he pulled the shower curtain back, even knowing their roommates could walk in on them at any moment? Maybe it was true that gay love could simply never be as wholesome as normal love. We wouldn't have to be so kinky, though, if only we could have actual sex, instead of practicing sexual circumlocution. Even within the bounds of celibacy, Elder Grant and I needed to live a lifetime in just a few months.

I didn't think I could stop wanting more and more of my companion. Homosexuality was clearly a progressive abomination, like cancer. We must already be at Stage Three. Once we reached Stage Four depravity, no treatment in existence had the power to save us.

If only we could be sure we would be sent to Outer Darkness together.

I looked across the room but was unable to detect even a vague outline of Elder Grant's bed.

Would it be better to see him in the Telestial Kingdom for eternity, or—magari—the Terrestrial, even if we were unable to touch each other intimately again…ever?

Elder Grant made a sudden whimpering sound, like a dog caught in a pyroclastic flow. A few moments later, he was breathing steadily again.

I wondered if I should suicidarmi to save him. Maybe he'd get back on the strait and narrow if I weren't around to drag him away from the iron rod. I couldn't just go back to America because he might follow. Or I might be pressured to tell someone why I'd left, and Elder Grant's life would be ruined.

I could pray for another earthquake, but that would affect so many other people, too.

Could I provoke one of the young punks in Sister Coticelli's neighborhood? Look for those sailors again and taunt them? Go back to that disturbing funicolare stop?

I knew the gospel was expressly designed for the spiritually sick. We were told in the MTC that if the only person we converted on our mission was ourselves, then the mission would be a success.

Perhaps I could become a truly bold messenger of the gospel and incite someone to martyr me.

My companion whimpered again.

What if Elder Murdock popped in before our alarm went off and found us together?

My cot creaked as I pulled myself to my feet. I carried my desk chair over beside Elder Grant's bed and sat down. Leaning over, I placed my head on his abdomen. He whimpered once again, felt around, barely awake, and stroked my hair a few times before falling back asleep.

Chapter Eleven:
Father, I Have Sinned

I found Vomero's middle class comfort comforting. It made me believe life could return to normal again someday. Class distinctions in Italy seemed different from those in the States, though. In Napoli, for instance, there had to be, at a minimum, five or six classifications of poverty.

How many classifications of normal might there be?

Elder Grant and I had knocked on every door in three palazzi in a row without success. But as we descended to the second floor in the next building, a middle-aged woman in a tight dress with a cheery floral print gave us a referral.

"I'm not interested," she told us, nervously rubbing an orange lily near her left breast, "but there's a priest next door who seems to need something more than what he's got." She pointed two doors over. This building, like most, only had three apartments per floor, all with doors facing the stairwell.

"Can we use your name?" Elder Grant asked her.

The woman smiled and nodded. "Lucia," she said. "He'll know."

The melody I'd learned in Culture Capsule floated through my brain. "Sul mare luccica…"

"Grazie mille," I said.

"Niente."

She closed the door while Elder Grant and I gave each other a hopeful glance. Some companionships stayed intact for six or seven months, but only if they were performing well.

Elder Grant rang the priest's doorbell. We heard a muffled "Chi é?" from deep inside the apartment. It was repeated two more times before the priest, wearing black pants and a black shirt, but with no white collar, opened his door.

"Buona sera," I said. It was my turn to do the approach. "Your neighbor Lucia said you might be interested in our message." I smiled. "We're—"

The priest held up a hand, laughing. "Lucia's a bitch," he said. "Worst neighbor I've ever had."

"Uh…"

"But come on in. I'll act like I *am* interested, and that'll bug the crap out of her."

I was just guessing at some of the words, but I caught the overall gist. The man waved us in, and we followed. When he shut the door behind us, he turned two deadbolts and hooked a chain.

"Sit, sit," he said, motioning to a black leather sofa.

We did, the leather making a soothing, crunching sound, and Elder Grant pulled out his flip charts.

"Oh, no." The priest laughed. "We'll have none of that. But why don't we chat for a few minutes? Then after you leave, I'll head over to Lucia's apartment and tell her you cursed her because she didn't invite you in."

"Per caritá!" Elder Grant jumped to his feet. "You can't do that!"

"Calmati." The priest motioned for my companion to sit back down, which he did rather hesitantly. "I'll think of something appropriate." He smiled genially. "You do have a way to curse others, don't you? The evil eye or something? No religion can do without a good curse."

"We dust off our feet," I said.

"Anziano!"

The priest laughed again. "Beautiful." He shook his head, still smiling. "We're all really the same underneath, aren't we?"

Elder Grant frowned and looked at me for a moment. He fingered his flip charts, his hand then moving to toy with his scratched nametag.

"Can I get you boys anything?" the priest asked. "Coffee? A glass of wine?" You weren't accountable for breaking the Word of Wisdom if you didn't know about the Word of Wisdom.

But how did Catholic priests relieve the stress of abstinence? "Padre," I began.

"Arpaia."

"Padre Arpaia," I started over, "can you take confession from someone who isn't a member of your church?"

"Flip!" Elder Grant shouted in English. "Pick!"

"Is something troubling you?" Father Arpaia asked in a voice that suddenly became gentle. He almost sounded sincere, though I suspected a patronizing indulgence. When he leaned forward in his black leather chair across from the sofa, it crunched comfortably. "Is there no one you can talk to at your church?" he went on. "Someone who will understand your situation better?"

"Well…" I began but stopped myself. It wasn't fair to talk about this without clearing it with my companion first. I looked at him and, after a moment, he closed his eyes and nodded. "It's just—"

"We can't let anyone at our church know what we've done," Elder Grant broke in. His eyes darted about the room as if he was expecting Elder Murdock or President Alsop to jump out from behind a chair.

"You converted rather quickly to the idea," Father Arpaia said, chuckling as he evaluated my companion. Elder Grant leaned back on the sofa, his arms folded across his chest.

"We—we've done something we weren't supposed to do," I said.

"Who doesn't?" His eyes traveled from my companion's face to mine and back to his. "And you've committed this sin more than once?"

Elder Grant looked at the floor, so Father Arpaia directed his attention back to me. Neither of us wanted to meet the priest's gaze, but I had talked to my bishop back home about masturbating half a dozen times before I sent off my mission papers, and I knew it had to be done.

"We masturbated together," I said, my voice squeaking in an irritating pitch. I shifted on the sofa, listening to the much nicer sound of the leather. I remembered watching previews back home for a film starring Al Pacino my second semester in college. Something called *Cruising*, if I remembered correctly. I'd viewed a clip of Pacino in leather and knew instinctively I couldn't allow myself to see such an inappropriate movie right before heading off to Provo. I'd even stoically refused to watch the in-flight movie over the Atlantic to Rome. *Fame*. No leather, but I knew it showcased an openly gay student.

When we played Irene Cara at the radio station in Quartu, I regretted those ascetic decisions, all the while avoiding lapses into self-abuse. I hadn't masturbated once the first several months of my mission. It wasn't until I heard Elder Grant's sheets rustling my first days in Napoli 2 that I'd succumbed again.

The idea of men in leather didn't scare me anymore, and that probably wasn't a good thing. I hadn't been ashamed when I was doing unspeakable things with my companion. But looking into Father Arpaia's face, I understood what Judgment Day was going to be like, when *everyone* would know *every* disgusting sin I'd ever committed. And liked.

I felt my dick hardening slightly at the prospect.

Goddammit.

Father Arpaia laughed. "Is that *all* you've done?" he asked.

I could feel my face burning and wondered briefly if "hellfire" was no more than an eternal sense of shame and embarrassment. Mormons didn't believe in a literal burning for eternity. My bishop had usually felt as uncomfortable as I had during our interviews and never asked any follow up questions. He wanted me out of his office as much as I wanted to leave. I wished I could run out of the priest's apartment now, but I knew that talking to the mission president in Rome or my stake president back in New Orleans would be far worse. And I *did* feel a slight thrill at the idea of exposing what we'd done. But mostly, I hoped he could help. Since I held the Melchizedek priesthood, the consequences for any level of sexual sin were heavier. Maybe, even if this guy didn't have the real priesthood, he could do something…say something…

"When Anziano Mortensen beats off," Elder Grant said, his arms still folded, "I lick the cum from his hand."

Still avoiding Father Arpaia's eyes, he shifted on the sofa, the sound driving me crazy. "And then he eats mine."

The priest stopped laughing. "But you just masturbate?" he asked slowly. "You don't have intercourse?"

"That's right," I said.

Father Arpaia looked at us both again, turned to contemplate a crucifix on his wall, and then seemed to study an ornately framed print, a religious painting I thought I remembered from the museum at Capodimonte. Two women were holding down a man and trying to cut off his head.

My bishop back home had paintings of flowery paths and sun-drenched mountain lakes in his living room.

I'd always wanted Arnold Friburg's Nephites on my walls.

"Do you guys love each other?" Father Arpaia asked abruptly. "Or are you just horny?"

"Uh…"

"I took a vow of celibacy twenty years ago," the priest continued, "and I've never violated it once." He stopped and glanced toward his apartment door. "Lucia…" he began but then held up a hand.

Elder Grant frowned.

"Do you guys love each other?" Father Arpaia repeated.

"Yes," I said. "I love him completely." I turned to look at my companion. "Even when he has morning breath." I offered a weak smile.

"I—I love him, too," Elder Grant said. He reached over to grab my hand.

Father Arpaia sighed. "Then the only real sin you're committing is not giving yourselves to each other fully. God doesn't want you to be lukewarm." He quoted Revelation 3:16 and then stood up. I realized our visit was over.

Were we supposed to tip him? Ask for some holy water?

"Is there…is there something we can pray?" I asked. "Some kind of penance?" Elder Grant and I certainly weren't going to become full-fledged lovers. The fact that Father Arpaia even suggested it proved the Catholic Church was in a deeply fallen state. We'd been told in the MTC that the Catholic Church was the whore of Babylon.

Though they disapproved of homosexuality, too, didn't they?

So…

I hated all this spaccacervello.

"Say a couple of Hail Marys tonight before you make love," he said, "and then thank God afterward for bringing

164

you together." He unlocked the two deadbolts and unhooked the chain.

"Thank you, Father," Elder Grant said, shaking his hand but still not looking the priest in the eye.

Father Arpaia examined his hand briefly as if checking to see if my companion had left some kind of residue. "The term is 'dusting your feet,' right?" he asked, looking past us toward his neighbor's door.

"Why don't you give her some flowers, Father?" I wrote down the name and street corner where Sister Longobardi had her flower stand. "Even if you can't love someone fully, sometimes it's still good to love them just a little."

Father Arpaia took the slip of paper, his brows furrowed, and shut his door.

***

"Anziano," I said as we stepped out on the sidewalk, startling something in the gutter, "how are we going to get home? The sciopero won't be over till tomorrow." It had been on my mind the last half hour, making it difficult to feel the Spirit until I decided to postpone worrying until after the closing prayer.

Elder Grant looked at his watch. "Caspita! I forgot."

I'd been no more willing to turn down an opportunity to teach that last discussion than he had. Two families in one evening. I'd only managed that once before on my mission. "Any members live near here?" Perhaps someone could give us a ride. We weren't technically supposed to ride with members, of course. Something about insurance. But under the circumstances, it might be worth the risk.

"Hmm." Elder Grant bit his lower lip. "There's Sorella Rizzi," he said, "and Sorella Cuomo. But they're single women."

"How about the Folvinis?" I asked.

"They don't have a car."

We stood on the sidewalk thinking for a few more minutes. I pulled my companion a little farther from the curb when I heard more rustling. Even in a nice area like this, there were sometimes newspapers in the gutter. But since there was no wind, I didn't want to know what other unseen force might be causing the sound. It wasn't all that cold, I realized. If we chose someplace off the ground, we could probably sleep in the park on neighboring benches if we had to. But if anyone saw two "homeless" missionaries, it might make the Church look bad. The whole region was still struggling with housing for the quarter of a million people displaced during the earthquake. We didn't want to look like part of the problem.

It wasn't only a matter of avoiding the appearance of evil, of course. There was also the appearance of incompetence, of weakness, of flaws of any kind.

The previous week, Elder Grant had dragged me to the office of a urologist and made an appointment for me. At first, I thought it had something to do with the most recent addition to our masturbation sessions, using our basters to squirt urine up each other's ass. My companion had also finally managed another evening to get his entire hand inside me. But I didn't see how either act required the consultation of a urologist. "We really need to see a psychiatrist," he explained, "but how would that look? We can't let people think less of the Church because of our own personal failures."

"You're not a failure."

"It wouldn't even matter if people never found out we were seeing someone about our homosexuality. *Whatever* problem they suspected would make them think less of the Church."

"And the urologist?" I'd asked.

Elder Grant had shrugged. "He's got to know *something* about dicks. Maybe he can help, and maybe he can't, but where else can we go?"

On the day of the appointment, we only made it as far as the waiting room. A middle-aged man reading a *Gente* sat on one side of us while an elderly man staring at the floor sat across the room. When the doctor opened a door and called for the middle-aged man, Elder Grant had a panic attack and ran out of the building. He still hadn't returned thirty minutes later when the middle-aged man departed with the elderly man and the doctor called for me.

Not sure he'd be able to help even if I managed to open up to him, I suddenly realized I couldn't face disrobing in his presence, if for some reason he asked to examine me. It felt like infidelity. I apologized and made my way outside.

My companion was waiting for me several yards down the street. "How'd it go?" he asked nervously.

"The doctor says we're perfectly normal."

Elder Grant had frowned, absentmindedly tapping the wallet in his front pocket. I'd been the one to pay for the appointment, though.

He was tapping his wallet again now.

Was getting a ride tonight from one of the sisters in the branch really the end of the world?

"Ho un'idea," Elder Grant said, putting a hand on my shoulder.

"Sí?"

"Let's find a cheap hotel."

My heart jumped instantly at the implications. "We don't have that kind of money," I protested. Not anymore.

"My Uncle Stuart said if I ever needed emergency money, he'd cover it." Elder Grant squeezed my shoulder comfortingly, but I still think I frowned. Why had he never mentioned this source of funding before?

Because admission to Pompeii wasn't an emergency. Lasagna for Elisabetta wasn't an emergency. Vongole for Luigi wasn't an emergency.

"Is *this* an emergency?" It would be cheaper to call a taxi. But if spending the night alone together felt like an emergency to my companion, then...

"I know where there's a hotel not far from here."

Which could only mean this wasn't the first time the idea had occurred to him.

"Venga." Elder Grant waved for me to follow. I wasn't going to turn down a soft bed and a chance to share more than a cot with my companion, so I started after him. Six blocks away, on Vico Mastellone, he pointed to a sign. Vista di Vesuvio. Of course, the view of the volcano was no better from here than from most other parts of the city. Elder Grant held the door open for me, and I entered.

The front desk clerk, not much older than we were, checked us in without setting down his cigarette. His eyes were slightly bloodshot, as if his capillaries thought it was the middle of the night. Elder Grant took the key and we headed upstairs to the first floor. Watching my companion turn the key and push the door open felt more thrilling, and scarier, than slipping naked under a sheet in the temple to get my initiatory.

The room smelled of smoke and something else I couldn't identify. The bed had been made, but some wrinkles on the cover suggested someone had set something down on it since. As cheap as this place was, though, at least we had our own bathroom, something we wouldn't have enjoyed if we'd checked into an even cheaper hostel.

"No biscotti this evening," Elder Grant said with a shrug.

"We'd better call the zone leaders and tell them what's up."

Elder Grant pulled a card out of his White Bible and picked up the heavy receiver on the bedstand. The phone back in our apartment was in the living room, which the zone leaders used as a bedroom. It was almost 10:20. Elder Murdock picked up immediately.

I went to the bathroom and took off my clothes while my companion tried to sound convincing. When I heard him hang up, I turned the water on in the shower. A moment later, Elder Grant came in and removed his clothing as well.

Why did this dumpy hotel room feel more sacred than the dressing room in the temple?

I stepped into the shower first and held out my hand. Despite the warm water, we were both trembling. We'd seen each other naked dozens of times. And we were safe from intrusion. We should have felt *less* nervous.

Elder Grant picked up a bar of soap, but instead of rubbing it against his body, he began rubbing it against mine. Across my arms, under my armpits, over my chest and back, down my ass, along my legs as well, and back up again. Everywhere but my penis. He let me lather that up myself and then took the soap back.

My companion set the bar down and shook his head when I reached to pick it up. He pulled me away from the stream of water and rubbed his hands briskly all over me, trying to get the soap to lather even more. Then he nodded. "Tocca ora a te." After dragging the bar across most of his body, I ventured a little closer to his penis, rubbing the bar over his balls again and again, but even I knew his actual dick was still off limits.

Maybe if I did it fast...

Who wanted to do it fast?

Standing on the far side of the tub to avoid rinsing our suds off too quickly, we hugged, Elder Grant sliding his nipples across mine. Our groins pressed together, and in seconds, I realized we needed to change our positions. I turned Elder Grant around and hugged him from behind. But feeling his slippery ass against my slick cock, I knew I couldn't maintain this position for long, either.

It would be so easy to slide it inside him. It would feel so smooth, so warm. So *good*.

How wonderful to touch one another at our leisure, knowing no other elders could come barging in. There was no need to feel hurried or frenzied, despite the limited hot water.

This must be what marriage was like.

"We should go to bed now," I said. "It's late."

We rinsed one another in the warm spray and then toweled each other off as well. Elder Grant kneeled to dry my calves and feet, his face only inches from my penis.

It was erect. How could it not be? My companion glanced at it, looked up at me, and resumed drying my legs.

I wanted to grab him by the hair.

When he stood a moment later, I wanted to grab him by his own erect penis.

We turned off the lights and slid under the covers, still naked. Elder Grant turned onto his side and backed up against me, pressing his ass against my crotch. I held onto him with one arm across his chest, pulling him even closer. He reached behind him and placed the tip of my dick against his hole.

"No one will know," he whispered.

He hadn't even finished the sentence before I started pushing forward. But our bodies were no longer slick and soapy. I thought about jumping out of bed to grab the consecrated oil from my keychain, and then the reality of what we were about to do hit me.

"Heavenly Father will know." I paused a moment. "We need to remember I Corinthians 10:13." Even as I said it, I realized I no longer found that scripture comforting. Several other verses drifted past my mind as well, but they didn't seem to help anymore, either.

I could feel my companion trembling next to me even more than before. When I pulled him tight against me, however, I realized he wasn't trembling.

"Non piangere," I whispered. "Please don't cry."

"If we actually *had* the Second Anointing…" he began but couldn't go on.

We could never get the Second Anointing, I realized, if we only wanted it so we could sin without consequence.

Spaccaanima.

Elder Grant's shoulders continued to shake, and I kissed his back gently. Finally, after another few minutes, he coughed, spluttered, and then caught his breath again.

"What in the world is going to become of us?" He sniffled and coughed once more.

I didn't know if he was asking me, asking God, or asking no one at all.

***

Elder Grant and I retired to our bedroom after the Transfer meeting. He caressed my forehead, and I raised his other hand to my lips.

"I…I…" he began. "We…" He shook his head.

Thank God, thank *God*, I'd asked my companion not to lick off his cum last night after he shot onto my face, so I could fall asleep smelling him on me.

He was heading for Sassari. I'd been there once with the ZLs in Sardinia. Sassari was in the middle of nowhere. Elder Wynn had tried to escape last year and was caught at the ferry terminal in Cagliari. The ZLs had asked Elder Cornett and me to accompany them as they brought him back to his companion. For some reason, they'd thought I'd be able to tell him something encouraging. Because he was from Virginia and we were both Southerners?

Wynn had committed suicide a month later. No one, naturally, ever talked about it.

I wondered what the mission president told his parents.

While my companion would be catching the ferry for Cagliari tomorrow morning, I'd be catching a train for Pescara. President Alsop still didn't seem to know the truth, but clearly Heavenly Father did.

"I want to punch myself," Elder Grant said, "slap myself, cut myself." He closed his eyes and shook his head vigorously. I knew that the pain he felt came from the realization he was causing *me* pain. I knew, because the only pain I felt right now was understanding the pain I was causing him.

Spaccacuore.

"Have some self-compassion, Anziano," I said so softly I could barely hear myself. "How would you treat 'you' if 'you' were a good friend?"

His eyes watered but he didn't cry.

I put my hand on his cheek and nodded. How could Ali McGraw have gotten it so wrong? "Love means always having to say you're sorry."

***

"I understand," Sister Coticelli said softly a few hours later, her smile calm. "I knew during that first dinner our time was going to be short." She laughed, but not with any bitterness. "You *have* to know by now I'm used to temporary."

It wasn't fair that the visits I'd hoped would bring her comfort might end up causing her more pain. "I'm sorry to have given you so few pleasant memories." At least, I hoped they were as pleasant for her as they were for me. But I wasn't sure if I wanted them to be enduring. Sometimes, forgetting minimized the grief.

"*I'm* not sorry."

"They don't usually send both elders away at the same time," Elder Grant let her know.

It meant no one would be stopping by again.

"Tutto bene." She raised the bottle of Acqua Ferrarelle I'd brought. Elder Grant and I raised bottles, too, and we all took a sip together. "I've decided to volunteer at the liceo near here." She smiled. "Tutor the kids who are still having trouble reading." She took another sip, closing her eyes to concentrate on the flavor. "If they can get a decent education, maybe they won't be trapped."

"Elisabetta," I said, "you're the second-best thing about my time in Napoli."

Elder Grant gasped at my obvious slight.

But Sister Coticelli laughed again. "I've been preparing for today." She opened a drawer in a bureau and pulled something out. "I got something to help you remember Napoli." She held up a couple of postcards showing frescoes from Pompeii, presenting one to Elder Grant. My companion stared at the god Priapus against a light blue background. Into my hands, Elisabetta placed the fresco of Priapus against a yellow background, with his impossibly, monstrously huge penis.

"Madonna!" my companion exclaimed before clapping a hand over his mouth.

Sister Coticelli smiled.

"Thank you, Elisabetta," I said, pulling her into a tight embrace. Hugging women was still against the rules.

"Thank *you*, ragazzi." She embraced Elder Grant, too, and kissed us both on our cheeks. "I'll be praying the rosary for you."

Chapter Twelve:
Mission Reunion

Three weeks ago, I received an email at work with the subject line, "Un amicone dal tuo passato." Elder Grant, now just plain old Gareth, had Googled me, discovered where I worked, and asked if I planned to attend our mission reunion in Salt Lake during General Conference.

We hadn't spoken in almost forty years.

Neither of us had ever attended any of our mission reunions before, and not only because we both lived outside of Utah. A few years ago, I'd been invited to join a closed Facebook group created for the missionaries who'd served under President Alsop.

I'd declined.

Caroline had never understood why, since I spoke so beautifully about those days, the few times I did speak about them. On our thirty-fifth anniversary, shortly before her diagnosis, I'd run my first full marathon, dedicating it to her in an attempt to make some kind of amends for my many secrets.

Caroline died eight months ago from colon cancer. She'd been too embarrassed when symptoms first began appearing to go to the doctor right away, had never been able to face the mortification of a colonoscopy even when I had polyps of my own removed. "Just tell me you're okay," she said. "I don't need to know any details."

She certainly didn't need to know about the dildo I kept locked up in the bottom desk drawer of my office in the back of the house.

Steven, now 33, and Karen, 31, would never even tell their own families what kind of cancer their mother had. I hated that I'd reinforced the sense of shame that seemed an underlying theme of almost every talk at church.

But I was too ashamed to get help.

Until after Caroline's death. By then, the work necessary to help my kids was more than I could face. I could barely even look myself in the mirror. Angry that my parents had allowed me to become more devout than they were, I was even angrier that I'd encouraged my children to become more devout than I'd ever been. But after two counseling sessions a week for the past half year, I could at least finally go to the library and check out movies I'd denied myself for decades: *Trick*, *Bound*, *Shortbus*, *3*, *Le fate ignoranti*. And, of course, *Latter Days* and *Milk*, which I'd especially avoided since they'd both been written by gay Mormons. For years, I vowed that if I couldn't watch them with Elder Grant, I didn't want to watch them at all.

Ma la vita va avanti.

I waited a week before replying to Gareth's email. "It will be so good to see you again," I wrote. "I hope with all my heart you've had a good, happy life." It was what I dreaded most of all as well.

I felt ashamed again.

Elder Grant replied to my reply before the end of that day. "My wife left me for a nun she met while volunteering at an interfaith hospice." The news could have made me happy, and to a degree it did, but for her, not for him.

"Karma's a bitch," I wrote back, "isn't it?" I told him about my own payback over the years, mysteriously developing oral syphilis a week after having my wisdom teeth extracted in my early twenties, receiving a concussion while breaking up a gay bashing during a walk through the French Quarter one afternoon with my family. I then related what I hoped were some funny moments and sweet experiences with my wife and kids over the past few decades before telling Gareth I was no longer married. "Sono vedovo."

I remembered Luigi.

"But, Scott, weren't you married in the temple?"

I'd genuinely loved Caroline. She had baked homemade cookies from her mother's recipe almost every week for the past two decades and brought them to a local soup kitchen, one batch for the workers and volunteers, another for the hungry folks who came for assistance, so they could do more than merely survive. Both our kids had gone on missions, Steven to Japan and Karen to Ireland.

Karen had even participated in Girls State back in high school. Married for less than two years now, she'd chosen to adopt a five-year-old mixed-race girl to start her forever family.

I was never sure, of course, if she'd adopted because even as a married woman, she felt sex was somehow still tainted.

When my daughter was a teenager, the bishop had called me into his office one evening to inform me that she had confessed to masturbation. "Bishop," I'd told him slowly and carefully, "Steven is two years older than Karen, and you've never felt the need to break any confidentiality regarding *his* worthiness interviews."

And yet I'd still attended services every week with my family after that.

I understood now how Elisabetta felt.

While I'd never criticized my children over any of their weaknesses, sexual or otherwise, I didn't need to. Bringing them to church assured they'd have all the instruction necessary to take care of that themselves.

So much time, I thought, trying to atone for the things I'd done on my mission, but all the while doing more harm.

It wasn't until Karen adopted her daughter that I realized a truth I wished I still didn't know: loving my kids didn't mean bringing them into the world had been the right thing to do. If that were the case, loving every child born to polygamous wives would justify polygamy. Loving a child conceived from rape would justify rape.

Loving Caroline had been the justification for not loving Elder Grant.

I emailed Gareth my phone number. He called an hour later. Just as the smell of cinnamon could transport a person back to a childhood holiday in their beloved grandmother's kitchen, the sound of my former companion's voice erased three dozen years. I told him our old address on Via Nicolardi. He told me the bus numbers of the routes we took most often.

"I sent a few postcards to Elisabetta whenever my family went on vacation," I said. In a more subdued voice, I added, "She died six years ago." And now I felt old again.

"I watch MHz on cable," Gareth said after a long pause.

"Ah," I said, understanding immediately. I'd never been able to get into Italian horror movies. I'd tried to keep up the language with a few Italo Calvino books and all the Aldo Busi I could find, but it was the mysteries and crime shows of the past few years that made me feel I was back where I belonged. "*Detective Montalbano. Murders at Barlume. Inspector Manara.*"

"*Bulletproof Heart*," he added. "*Nero Wolfe.*"

I paused. "*I Bastardi di Pizzofalcone.*"

Gareth paused as well. "Yes, that's when I knew I was going to have to call you sooner or later." He sighed. "That was two years ago."

"Ah," I breathed again. "A full-time mission ago." The line was silent once more.

"I didn't go to the temple dedication in Rome last year."

"Neither did I."

"I still have a recommend."

"I threw mine away the day I got your first email."

"Oh, Anziano."

Gareth and I talked on the phone every night after that first conversation. He explained why he hadn't sent me a wedding invitation all those years ago, and I explained why I hadn't looked him up during a family trip to San Francisco. He told me about the one time he cheated on Shawna with another man, how grateful he'd been that she forgave him. I wanted to tell him I forgave him, too, but I had nothing to forgive.

"She was a great wife," he went on. "We tried a good many things I expect other women in the Church wouldn't."

Was he talking about pegging? Caroline had pretty much only wanted sex once a month, on Fast Sunday when neither of us had the energy to try anything daring.

"Can I ask?"

"Oh, you know, white water rafting, horse riding, a little skydiving."

I laughed.

"She even took up scuba diving, but that was too scary for me."

When we saw each other in the conference room at the Marriott this afternoon, we ran toward one another as if fleeing a cloud of ash, slamming into each other with open arms.

I hoped someone had their phone out. I wanted to put that scene in slow motion and add a song by Laura Pausini to the soundtrack.

"Le cose che vivi."

But if anyone was filming, they stopped the moment Gareth planted his lips on mine. I heard someone unknowingly quote a line from *Starman*: "Every gosh darn place you go…"

Well, what passed for a direct quote from someone who probably still watched *That Darn Cat* and *The Computer Wore Tennis Shoes*.

In all likelihood the inspiration for the *Tennis Shoes among the Nephites* series.

Elisabetta had taught me that life was better without bitterness.

"Tu sei l'uomo piú bello che abbia mai visto," Gareth told me.

"Everybody's throwing around hyperbole these days," I replied, shaking my head. "I think this is the most hyperbolic time *ever.*"

Gareth smiled. "Damn, I've missed you."

My old companion and I left immediately for my hotel room upstairs. He was attractive in that old-man-next-door kind of way. The kind of friendly neighbor, perhaps, who had a sling in his basement, who might invite you downstairs wearing a black leather armband along with his white T-shirt. After hours and hours of conversation over the past couple of weeks, we no longer needed time to get reacquainted. I pulled off my suit coat and tie, kicked off my shoes, and unbuttoned my shirt.

Soon, Gareth stood before me in an old pair of his one-piece garments. The Church had been selling two-piece varieties since the time we'd come home.

"I had to lose a little weight to fit in them again," Gareth confessed, patting his slightly protruding belly. I could see the ancient, dried cum I'd left for him as a farewell all those years ago. "I kept my San Gennaro, too," he added.

"I've got my wooden inlay portrait of you on my desk at work."

When I finished undressing a moment later, Gareth smiled to see I was wearing the garments on which he'd deposited his own parting gift our last day together. I'd never washed mine, either, had kept them in a velvet pouch meant for temple clothes, in a box Caroline instinctively sensed she should never look inside. Every year on my companion's birthday, I'd taken them out and pressed them against my face. I pulled them down over my shoulders now to my waist.

"A nipple ring, huh?" he asked, fingering it gently.

I'd only taken Steven and Karen to Mardi Gras parades in Metairie as they were growing up, never those on Canal Street or St. Charles Avenue. The one time Caroline had taken the kids to visit her mother in Chattanooga during the school break, I'd ventured into the French Quarter on my own. What I'd witnessed on a wide corner balcony on Burgundy had made me ache for my old companion even more than listening to Claudio Baglioni in the dark.

"Wait'll you see me in my leather vest." I'd purchased some leather porn a few days after Elder Grant and I started calling each other, and I'd studied up on pissing and fisting. But really, all I wanted to do, over and over and over, was make love in the simplest and purest way possible.

We kissed again. I'd forgotten how wonderful Elder Grant was with his tongue. I pulled away and placed a bottle of hair conditioner on the bedside table. My old CD player was already in place, and I pushed Play. Dario Beldan Bembo began singing a song we'd first heard through the wall from our neighbor's radio the P-Day after our trip to Pompeii.

"Tu cosa fai stasera?"

Gareth lay face down on the bed, and I lay on top of him, kissing the back of his neck gently. I pried open the slit in the seat of his garments and placed a huge dab of conditioner along my shaft. "I wish…" I began. "I wish I had done this four decades ago."

"If you had," Gareth whispered, "maybe…"

"There's no more time for maybes," I said. "I've already arranged to meet with an Episcopal priest here in Salt Lake who will marry us."

"Shouldn't you be on your knees when you propose to me?"

"As opposed to on your back?"

"What will we tell the grandkids?" He laughed.

But I didn't.

"Scott." My companion turned his head sideways against the mattress to look up at me. "My kids are getting used to seeing their mother with another woman. They'll be able to handle us together sooner or later, too."

I kissed his cheek. Then the back of his neck again. Then his shoulders. "I'm afraid my children will be the kind of members who never accept us." Caroline and I had taught them far too well the importance of following the Prophet.

Spaccafamiglia.

"Scott…"

"It's okay. I've postponed the life I want long enough." I kissed the middle of his back, his lower back, both ass cheeks. "If God can't be good to us now, why would he be good to us after we die?" I spread his cheeks and kissed his asshole. "Caro, I'm going to spend the rest of my life with you." Eternity, if there was such a thing, I'd worry about later. I reached again for my hair conditioner and applied a healthy dab on his hole, rubbing my finger along the edges. "Va bene?" I asked. "Sarai il mio marito?"

I carefully pressed the head of my penis past his sphincter, let him adjust for a moment, and then slid my fat cock all the way inside his hot ass, and I knew, for the first time, what being one with the universe meant. May the Force be with us, I prayed.

Gareth moaned as I started pumping. Making love with him felt as thrilling as the first time and yet as comforting as maintenance sex an old couple might perform on their fiftieth wedding anniversary. Not everyone had died in Pompeii, I realized. Some people had made it out. "Yes," he said, and I realized I'd never heard a lovelier word either in English or Italian. "My answer is yes."

Books by Johnny Townsend

Thanks for reading! If you enjoyed this book, could you please take a few minutes to write a review online? Reviews are helpful both to me as an author and to other readers, so we'd all sincerely appreciate your writing one! And if you did enjoy the book, here are some others I've written you might want to look up:

Mormon Underwear

God's Gargoyles

The Circumcision of God

Sex among the Saints

Dinosaur Perversions

Zombies for Jesus

The Abominable Gayman

The Gay Mormon Quilter's Club

The Golem of Rabbi Loew

Mormon Fairy Tales

Flying over Babel

Marginal Mormons

Mormon Bullies

The Mormon Victorian Society

Dragons of the Book of Mormon

Selling the City of Enoch

A Day at the Temple

Behind the Zion Curtain

Gayrabian Nights

Lying for the Lord

Despots of Deseret

Missionaries Make the Best Companions

Invasion of the Spirit Snatchers

The Tyranny of Silence

Sex on the Sabbath

The Washing of Brains

The Mormon Inquisition

Interview with a Mission President

Weeping, Wailing, and Gnashing of Teeth

Behind the Bishop's Door

The Moat around Zion

The Last Days Linger

Mormon Madness

Human Compassion for Beginners

Dead Mankind Walking

Who Invited You to the Orgy?

Breaking the Promise of the Promised Land

I Will, Through the Veil

Am I My Planet's Keeper?

Have Your Cum and Eat It, Too

Strangers with Benefits

What Would Anne Frank Do?

This Is All Just Too Hard

Blessed Are the Firefighters

Wake Up and Smell the Missionaries

Racism by Proxy

Orgy at the STD Clinic

Life Is Better with Love

Please Evacuate

Let the Faggots Burn: The UpStairs Lounge Fire

Latter-Gay Saints: An Anthology of Gay Mormon Fiction (co-editor)

Available from BookLocker.com or your favorite online or neighborhood bookstore.

Wondering what some of those other books are about? Read on!

The Washing of Brains

A world-weary man becomes a widower for the third time. A non-Mormon couple allow their teenage daughter to be baptized but are then shocked when she rejects them and moves in with a more righteous family. A man awakens to celebrate a milestone birthday only to discover that horrifying world events demand his attention instead. A budding feminist tries to make a political statement by giving birth to her "illegitimate" son in church just before Mother's Day. Missionaries in Rome try to prevent a terrorist bombing. The Prophet devises a plan to reverse global warming. A Salt Lake bishop is overwhelmed by his congregants' secrets. A gay Mormon man devastated by the breakup of his marriage to a closeted Hasidic Jew considers returning to the fold. An unhappy bartender reminisces about the affair he had with his mission president in Paris. A returned missionary takes a job in an adult video store. A young woman befriends the dungeon master who lives above her. A BYU student working as an escort finds love.

Invasion of the Spirit Snatchers

During the Apocalypse, a group of Mormon survivors in Hurricane, Utah gather in the home of the Relief Society president, telling stories to pass the time as they ration their food storage and await the Second Coming. But this is no ordinary group of Mormons— or perhaps it is. They are the faithful, feminist, gay, apostate, and repentant, all working together to help each other through the darkest days any of them have yet seen.

Gayrabian Nights

Gayrabian Nights is a twist on the well-known classic, *1001 Arabian Nights*, in which Scheherazade, under the threat of death if she ceases to captivate King Shahryar's attention, enchants him through a series of mysterious, adventurous, and romantic tales.

In this variation, a male escort, invited to the hotel room of a closeted, homophobic Mormon senator, learns that the man is poised to vote on a piece of anti-gay legislation the following morning. To prevent him from sleeping, so that the exhausted senator will miss casting his vote on the Senate floor, the escort entertains him with stories of homophobia, celibacy, mixed orientation marriages, reparative therapy, coming out, first love, gay marriage, and long-term successful gay relationships. The escort crafts the stories to give the senator a crash course in gay culture and sensibilities, hoping to bring the man closer to accepting his own sexual orientation.

Let the Faggots Burn: The UpStairs Lounge Fire

On Gay Pride Day in 1973, someone set the entrance to a French Quarter gay bar on fire. In the terrible inferno that followed, thirty-two people lost their lives, including a third of the local congregation of the Metropolitan Community Church, their pastor burning to death halfway out a second-story window as he tried to claw his way to freedom. A mother who'd gone to the bar with her two gay sons died alongside them. A man who'd helped his friend escape first was found dead near the fire escape. Two children waited outside a movie theater across town for a father and step-father who would never pick them up. During this era of rampant homophobia, several families refused to claim the bodies, and many churches refused to bury the dead. Author Johnny Townsend pored through old records and tracked down survivors of the fire as well as relatives and friends of those killed to compile this fascinating account of a forgotten moment in gay history.

The Abominable Gayman

What is a gay Mormon missionary doing in Italy? He is trying to save his own soul as well as the souls of others. In these tales chronicling the two-year mission of Robert Anderson, we see a young man tormented by his inability to be the man the Church says he should be. In addition to his personal hell, Anderson faces a major earthquake, organized crime, a serious bus accident, and much more. He copes with horrendous mission leaders and his own suicidal tendencies. But one day, he meets another missionary who loves him, and his world changes forever.

Marginal Mormons

What happens when a High Priest becomes addicted to crack cocaine? Should an unemployed bank teller take in a homeless protester from the Occupy movement? Do gay people have positive near-death experiences or unhappy ones? Is there a way to splice the empathy gene into the genome of every human? Can a schizophrenic woman on anti-delusional drugs still keep her belief in an intangible God? Will a childless biochemist be able to find fulfillment by taking part in a mission to Mars? Should a stay-at-home mom become involved in an international protest against fracking? Not every Latter-day Saint has a mainstream story to tell, but these soul-searching people are still more than the marginal Mormons headquarters would like us to believe.

Missionaries Make the Best Companions

What lies behind the freshly scrubbed façades of the Mormon missionaries we see about town? In these stories, an ex-Mormon tries to seduce a faithful elder by showing him increasingly suggestive movies. A sister missionary fulfills her community service requirement by babysitting for a prostitute. Two elders break their mission rules by venturing into the forbidden French Quarter. A black Mormon deals with racism in the Church. A senior missionary couple try to reactivate lapsed members while their own family falls apart back home. A young man hopes that serving a second full-time mission will lead him up the Church hierarchy. Two bored missionaries decide to make a little extra money moonlighting in a male stripper club. Two frustrated elders find an acceptable way to masturbate—by donating to a Fertility Clinic. A lonely man searches for the favorite companion he hasn't seen in thirty years.

Dragons of the Book of Mormon

A supporter of Prop 8 is forced to attend his boss's gay wedding. A devout Latter-day Saint struggling to pay his bills wonders if he should keep paying tithing, even after being excommunicated. A reporter seeks the identity of Salt Lake's new superhero—a masked man wearing temple clothes who mysteriously shows up at crime scenes. A woman is murdered in the temple on her wedding day. A devoted husband loses his wife on their wedding anniversary. One of the Three Nephites is missing in Pasadena. Mormons survive the zombie apocalypse because of their two-year supply of food storage.

Mormon Underwear

Mormon Underwear tells the stories of gay Mormons that mainstream members don't want to hear. Whether it is a young LDS man stripping to his Mormon underwear in public or a virginal 70-year-old finally giving in to temptation, a straight son who discovers his father kissing another man or a group who plots to put gays into positions of power within the Church, these are the stories too shameful or shocking to be told among traditional Saints.

The Golem of Rabbi Loew

Jacob and Esau Cohen are the closest of brothers. In fact, they're lovers. A doctor tries to combine canine genes with those of Jews, to improve their chances of surviving a hostile world. A Talmudic scholar dates an escort. A scientist tries to develop the "God spot" in the brains of his patients in order to create a messiah. The Golem of Prague is really Rabbi Loew's secret lover. While some of the Jews in Townsend's book are Orthodox, this collection of Jewish stories most certainly is not.

The Mormon Victorian Society

A Victorian enthusiast has a startling sexual revelation to make at his monthly Society meeting. A father tries desperately to save his family from the imminent danger of global warming. Two men find love in the aftermath of Hurricane Katrina. A gay man attending his first Affirmation conference becomes embroiled in ex-Mormon politics. A home teaching assignment goes terribly wrong when a man whose father was murdered in a gay bar is confronted with a young gay cowboy. A Relief Society president is trapped on a plane next to a gay man flaunting his sexuality. A ministering angel to a young god tires of his position. Gay Mormons react when the Prophet has a new revelation about homosexuality.

Interview with a Mission President

Jason Kincaid is nearing the end of his three-year term as president of the Washington Seattle mission of the LDS Church. His service has been difficult, and for the first time in his life, he has doubts. During the last zone conference over which he presides, he does something he's never done before. In each of his interviews with the missionaries serving under him, he asks them to openly discuss their own doubts. He hopes that by building up their faith, he will rebuild his own.

What happens instead will rock the entire Church to its core.

The Last Days Linger

The scriptures tell us that in the Last Days, wickedness will increase upon the Earth. When leaders of the Mormon Church see a rise in the number of gay members, they believe the end is upon them. But while "wickedness never was happiness," it begins to appear that wickedness can sometimes be divine. At least, the stories here suggest that religious proscriptions condemning homosexuality have it all wrong. While gay Mormons may be no closer to perfection than anyone else, they're no further from it, either. And sometimes, being gay provides just the right ingredient to create saints—as flawed as God himself.

Mormon Madness

Mental illness can strike the faithful as easily as anyone else. But often religious doctrine and practice exacerbate rather than alleviate these problems. From schizophrenia to obsessive-compulsive disorder, from persecution complex to sexual dysfunction, autism to dissociative identity disorder, Mormons must cope with their mental as well as their spiritual health on a daily basis.

Breaking the Promise of the Promised Land: How Religious Conservatives Failed America

By aligning themselves over the past 60 years with the most conservative wing of the Republican Party, Mormons became leading contributors to the cultural and moral decay of America. Mormon prophets have long declared that God set America apart for the righteous. It was to be a land of freedom, justice, and peace, a place where the Lamanites could blossom as the rose, a country so righteous that the affairs of the entire world would be conducted here during the Millennium.

But when Mormons tired of being "a peculiar people" and chose to side with the most repressive evangelicals, they chose to make America the land of the imprisoned, poor, and oppressed. While declaring their allegiance to the Prince of Peace, they've chosen to support policies that have kept America at war almost non-stop for the last six decades.

Perhaps rather than continue following old men who tell them what an invisible God wants them to do, they should consider doing what they can see with their own eyes the people all around them need.

Am I My Planet's Keeper?

Global Warming. Climate Change. Climate Crisis. Climate Emergency. Whatever label we use, we are facing one of the greatest challenges to the survival of life as we know it.

But while addressing greenhouse gases is perhaps our most urgent need, it's not our only task. We must also address toxic waste, pollution, habitat destruction, and our other contributions to the world's sixth mass extinction event.

In order to do that, we must simultaneously address the unmet human needs that keep us distracted from deeper engagement in stabilizing our climate: moderating economic inequality, guaranteeing healthcare to all, and ensuring education for everyone.

And to accomplish *that*, we must unite to combat the monied forces that use fear, prejudice, and misinformation to manipulate us.

It's a daunting task. But success is our only option.

Have Your Cum and Eat It, Too

It's 1981, and two Mormon missionaries randomly assigned to work together as "companions" in Napoli find themselves in trouble. They're falling in love, but the Church forbids gay relationships. As missionaries, they can't date anyone at all, much less other men. If they're found out, they'll be excommunicated, sent home in disgrace, and cast out from their families.

In the aftermath of a devastating earthquake, against a backdrop of poverty and repressive mission culture, Elders Grant and Mortensen knock on doors, endure violent assaults, and face the ultimate challenge—will they be crushed by dedication to their beliefs or will love provide a way for them to escape?

Wake Up and Smell the Missionaries

Two Mormon missionaries in Italy discover they share the same rare ability—both can emit pheromones on demand. At first, they playfully compete in the hills of Frascati to see who can tempt "investigators" most. But soon they're targeting each other non-stop.

Can two immature young men learn to control their "superpower" to live a normal life…and develop genuine love? Even as their relationship is threatened by the attentions of another man?

They seem just on the verge of success when a massive earthquake leaves them trapped under the rubble of their apartment in Castellammare.

With night falling and temperatures dropping, can they dig themselves out in time to save themselves? And will their injuries destroy the ability that brought them together in the first place?

Orgy at the STD Clinic

Todd Tillotson is struggling to move on after his husband is killed in a hit and run attack a year earlier during a Black Lives Matter protest in Seattle.

In this novel set entirely on public transportation, we watch as Todd, isolated throughout the pandemic, battles desperation in his attempt to safely reconnect with the world.

Will he find love again, even casual friendship, or will he simply end up another crazy old man on the bus?

Things don't look good until a man whose face he can't even see sits down beside him despite the raging variants.

And asks him a question that will change his life.

Please Evacuate

A gay, partygoing New Yorker unconcerned about the future or the unsustainability of capitalism is hit by a truck and thrust into a straight man's body half a continent away. As Hunter tries to figure out what's happening, he's caught up in another disaster, a wildfire sweeping through a Colorado community, the flames overtaking him and several schoolchildren as they flee.

When he awakens, Hunter finds himself in the body of yet another man, this time in northern Italy, a former missionary about to marry a young Mormon woman. Still piecing together this new reality, and beginning to embrace his latest identity, Hunter fights for his life in a devastating flash flood along with his wife *and* his new husband.

He's an aging worker in drought-stricken Texas, a nurse at an assisted living facility in the direct path of a hurricane, an advocate for the unhoused during a freak Seattle blizzard.

We watch as Hunter is plunged into life after life, finally recognizing the futility of only looking out for #1 and understanding the part he must play in addressing the global climate crisis…if he ever gets another chance.

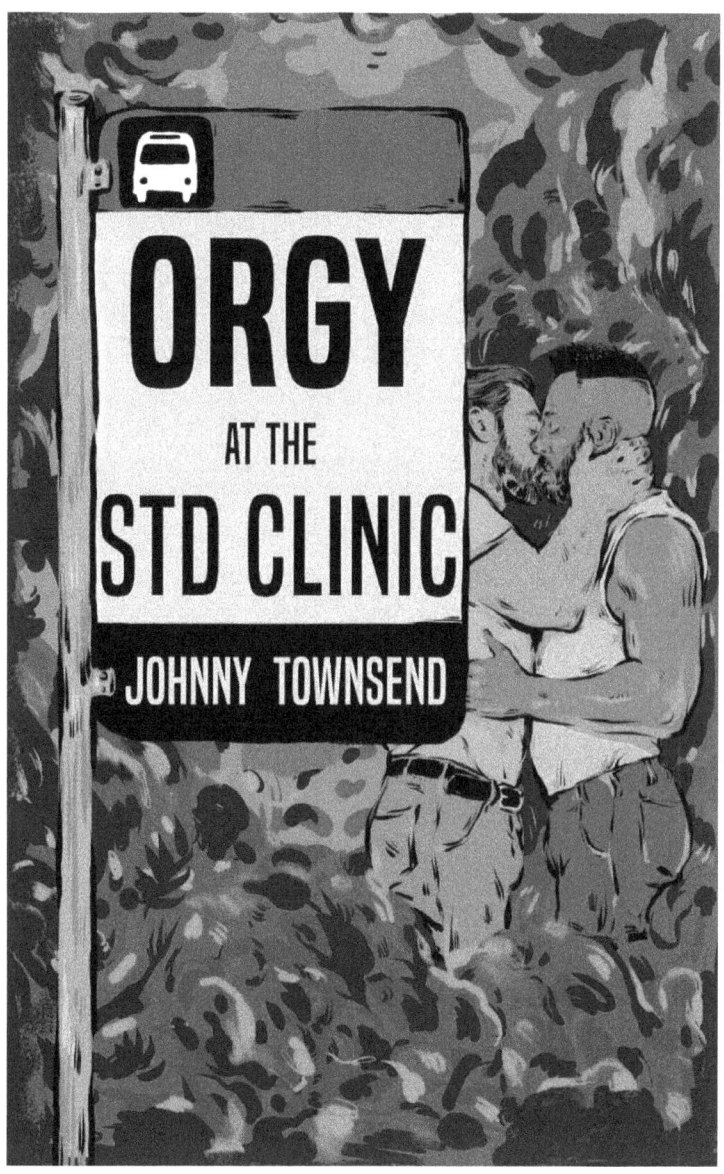

Chapter One from

Wake Up and Smell the Missionaries

"I'm not a superhero," I typed. "As you'll soon see, I'm not a hero at all. I wasn't bitten by a radioactive bug. I wasn't struck by lightning. I didn't even have a special hammer like Thor, only a vial of consecrated olive oil on my keychain so that as a Mormon priesthood holder, I'd be ready to bestow blessings whenever necessary."

"Are you really going to do it?" Brian asked, looking over my shoulder. "You're going to tell everyone our secret?"

"Afraid they'll lock us away?" I turned in my chair and pulled my husband close to give him a peck. Suddenly, without warning, I wanted nothing more than for him to take me on top of my desk. "Stop it," I said.

"You sure, Jeff?" He batted his eyes.

"Don't distract me while I'm writing our story."

He looked at me with a Mona Lisa smile.

"You're killing me," I groaned.

"OK, OK." He laughed, waving his hands in the air between us. "I'll open a window and let you get back to work."

I shut the door after he left my office, a spare bedroom looking out over the front pathway, and opened a bottle of rose perfume that I kept on a bookshelf for emergencies. One tiny sniff, then a moment leaning out the window to take in the forest air, and I started to calm down.

"Perhaps my DNA had simply undergone a random mutation," I typed. "I realized shortly after reaching adulthood that I had a special talent, a superpower that could be used for either good or not so good. Always a late bloomer, I was still young and immature, soon well on the road to becoming a supervillain, when on my first time through the temple, I had 'a vision' of that future and decided to change direction."

I stopped typing and looked at my computer screen. I hated including all the religious stuff, since I was no longer a believer. But I couldn't tell my story—*our* story—without it.

It was possible Brian was right, anyway. We were already seen as freaks by our families, by almost half of society. I remembered a scene from an episode of *La Porta Rossa* Brian and I had watched last night, when a teenage girl in Trieste discovers she can talk to a murdered police officer and is afraid her friends will think she's crazy.

"Some dogs can smell cancer," I continued typing. "A woman realized recently that she smelled her husband's Parkinson's disease years before he developed obvious symptoms, and she then went on to diagnose others. I've never had a particularly sensitive nose. What I did have, I discovered during my first year in college, was the ability to emit pheromones on command, a scent undetectable on a conscious level but which affected other people—other *men*—almost instantly."

I moved over to the window and looked outside. Brian and I had retired just before the pandemic started and moved to the outskirts of Roslyn. The smell of firs and cedars and spruces and redwoods was intoxicating. We spent a great deal of time outdoors even in the rain and snow.

Nature smelled good.

When it wasn't on fire.

I walked over to my office door and banged against it. "You stop that now, Brian," I said, trying to sound angry, "or I'm going to put a chip clip on your nose later while you suck me off!"

Most couples lost their lust for one another not long after their honeymoon period. But even after forty years, we were incapable of losing ours. So I couldn't complain *too* much.

"Oh, all right," I said, opening a speakeasy door at waist height and pulling my chair up next to it. Brian poked his erect dick through, I sucked him off, and finally, he left me in peace for a bit. I closed the speakeasy door and returned to my computer.

Neither of us had ever experienced a mid-life crisis because we were perpetual teenagers.

It was almost like having a resurrected body.

Except that the other day when I'd wiped the fog off the bathroom mirror to brush my teeth, I gasped at my reflection. "What?" asked Brian, peeking around the edge of the shower curtain.

"I'm losing telomeres right and left," I said.

Brian had stepped out of the shower and, without even drying off first, had hugged me from behind, kissing me on the neck. "I didn't fall in love with you for your telomeres," he whispered.

He'd pulled my boxer briefs down, grabbed some hair conditioner, and fucked me before returning to his shower.

And even though I *knew* that I knew the answer, I'd asked myself the same question every wealthy or beautiful or famous person did: Does he really like me for *me*?

Just as frightening was the accompanying question: Do I really like him for *him*?

"Turning other men on," I typed now, "might not seem like much of a gift to a young Mormon about to serve two years as a missionary, but it helped me find the man I'd spend the rest of my life with…and survive the night that almost killed us both."

Chapter One from *Please Evacuate*

I awoke from a nightmare in which I was drowning and found myself lying next to a naked woman. In the dim light, I could just make out the olive coloring of her skin and her thick, dark hair. The woman's nipples pointed toward the ceiling.

I screamed.

"What!?" The woman beside me sat up with her hand on her bare breasts. I'd never done drag, so I couldn't begin to guess their official size. But they were decidedly large. "What's wrong, honey?"

"Who are you?" I demanded. My eyes darted quickly about the room, the possibility that my dad was somehow behind this flashing insanely through my brain. I could just make out photos in large plastic frames on top of a dresser and a painting of a cow on the far wall. Not a gay man's bedroom.

What kind of folks *did* hang paintings of cows in their bedroom?

"Where am I?"

"Oh, honey!" The woman reached over to caress the side of my head. She had well-manicured nails, belying her taste in room décor, and her eyebrows were carefully plucked, suggesting a missing isthmus.

Was she trans? A sheet covered potentially useful information.

"Who are you?" I repeated.

"Are you serious?" Her eyes narrowed. "Do we need to get you to the hospital?"

I pulled away from the woman. The nightlight gave off enough of a glow to reveal the worry in her eyes, more suspicious than genuine.

But I'd never gone home with a woman before. Still a virgin at thirty-five as far as that was concerned.

Men, though, I'd awakened beside plenty of times over the past fifteen years. Never enough men, of course, but there were decades left to improve that tally.

The woman reached for me again and this time touched the back of my head. It hurt.

If this was PTSD, it was late in coming. I'd refused grief counseling after Dad's death.

"You think you have a concussion?" she asked. When I frowned, she returned the look. "You fell and hit your head," she explained, enunciating carefully, "when we were stepping out of the shower last night."

"I did?" I asked. "We…we showered together?" Had someone slipped me some LSD?

"Nick, you better not be jerking me around." The woman's lips tightened. I wondered if they'd been around my cock earlier. I wondered— "You promised to watch Jamie in the morning so I could do the building inspection."

"My name's not Nick."

The woman rolled her eyes. "For God's sake, are you role-playing again?" She stole a glance at the clock on the bedside table. "It's frickin' 3:00 in the morning."

"My name's Hunter," I said firmly.

"You sure it's not Peter? 'Cause you're being a dick. You know I don't like sex in the middle of the night."

"I don't want sex, either," I told her. I lifted the sheet to see that I was nude, too. How in the world was I going to get out of here?

Wherever here was.

"I want to go home."

At this, the woman's frown finally disappeared, replaced by a soft smile. "Little boy lost?" she suggested.

"I'm not little."

The woman reached for me under the sheet. "You are now but I can change that."

"Who are you?"

The woman's smile widened slightly. "Amnesia, huh? We haven't tried that one yet." She pulled the sheet up over her like a cape and straddled me. "Let me see if I can spark some memories."

Oh, I had memories. Dad giving me monthly testosterone injections starting on my thirteenth birthday. Him groaning every time he'd been forced to introduce me to a friend or acquaintance. "We should never have named you Hunter," he'd tell me afterward. "But no one wants to name their son Florist or Figure Skater."

For someone who didn't like sex in the middle of the night, the naked woman on top of me put in a valiant effort. Given my terror, confusion, and thorough lack of interest, it took a good three minutes before I grew hard and another five before I came.

Afterward, she rolled over and went to sleep. I did, too. Figured this was all a dream, anyway—at least a wet nightmare—and when I woke up later, I'd actually wake up.

I didn't.

I still seemed to be Nick and still didn't know this woman's name, afraid to ask since she'd written off my confusion earlier as a joke. I could hardly start guessing like Jerry Seinfeld had in an old rerun I'd once watched.

"Mulva?"

What if I used to be straight, I wondered, until I bumped my head? What if it was the *other* life I seemed to remember that was the dream? All those visions of dicks…maybe I was a urologist.

And what if the opposite had happened? I didn't think I'd ever been into S&M, but what if I used to be gay and some injury had turned me straight?

Mom had always said she hoped Dad could beat the gay away. I hadn't been charged when I pushed him in front of a gas truck during the last beating he ever gave me. We were on a father-son outing, planning to "rough it" in the woods, but we never reached the state park. When we stopped at a gas station to refuel, he caught me ogling the cashier.

Yikes.

What if *he'd* jumped into another life after I'd killed him and was now beating someone else's kid?

The woman beside me moaned as she slowly awakened. "Can you make sure the kids are up?" she mumbled.

"Sure…sweetie."

"Even Jamie. I know she's sick, but she needs to eat."

First, I headed to the bathroom, en suite so easy to find. I peed before daring to look in the mirror.

That definitely wasn't me. Just urinating a moment earlier had proven that, of course. The head of Nick's dick was larger than mine. Not quite a toadstool, but the instrument would be challenging for some guys to take.

Nick's nose was smaller than my own, almost narrow, his stubble so slight he probably only needed to shave every other day. His hair was straight and sandy, his ears flatter against the side of his head. Nice hair pattern on his chest.

Not bad, I thought, in a dad bod kind of way.

I caressed my right nipple and watched as my penis twitched.

Damn, I kind of wanted to have sex with that guy in the mirror.

Not the first time I realized I was a narcissist.

I slipped through the bedroom, the woman sitting groggily on the edge of the bed, and entered the hallway. Before anyone could catch my ignorance, I started opening doors and peeking inside.

"Rise and shine!"

Three kids. All I could find, at least.

I reached the kitchen first, wondering if I should scramble some eggs. But there weren't any in the fridge. I opened a cabinet and found four types of breakfast cereal. I set them all on the table, along with a stack of bowls and a jug of milk. Anticipating the needs of others wasn't really my forte, but I needed to deflect attention until I could figure out what was going on.

Alien experimentation?

Sometimes, dreams felt real until you woke up, and then you realized instantly how impossible they'd been. I didn't remember ever having a dream this vivid before, but then, who remembered dreams for more than a few minutes? It was impossible to know if they felt this real in the moment.

But I'd learned years ago how to take an active role in my dreams. If I didn't like the way the story was playing out, I would "rewind" the scene and do something different. That all seemed perfectly logical in the dream itself.

So I was a husband and dad for now. But if I was staying home from work today to take care of my sick daughter, perhaps I could give her some alcohol-based cold medicine and tell her to take a nap after everyone else left while I called a plumber or kept an eye out for the mail carrier for some extramarital play.

No point letting a dream go to waste.

As I poured myself some oatmeal crunch, I listened to the sound of the shower in the en suite and light footsteps in the hallway shuffling down to another bathroom. I started chomping on my cereal while trying to reconstruct the events of the previous evening.

Food had never tasted this real in a dream before.

Had it?

I took another bite and chomped some more. Perhaps someone had slipped Rohypnol into my drink last night and this was all a big practical joke. Or revenge for sleeping with someone's husband. A mad scientist's bizarre research project.

I couldn't finish the cereal.

Where were the damn kids?

I licked my spoon dry and struck my head with it several times. Was that a B flat? "Wake up!" I ordered myself out loud.

The last thing I remembered before finding myself in bed with a woman was strutting into a Lamborghini dealership to impress…what was his name?

Jonathan. An attorney I'd met at a professionals bar in Manhattan. We'd gone out a time or two, he had a big dick and a gifted tongue, and I wanted to prove my competitive worth despite my smaller dick.

Slightly smaller.

"You live in Chelsea and you want to buy a gas guzzler like that?"

I wasn't sure what kind of law Jonathan specialized in. When he started talking about environmental justice, my eyes glazed over.

"We could zip up to the Hamptons," I said. "Or spend a weekend in Montreal."

"We could take a train," he countered, "or rent a more reasonable car."

The conversation had deteriorated quickly after that. Jonathan began acting all holier-than-thou and I decided I could find a guy with an even bigger dick and more gifted tongue if I started cruising around in a Lamborghini. I'd just been promoted, after all, my new office providing a great view of the Hudson. No reason not to live life to the fullest.

It was time to trade in my Jag anyway.

The last thing I remembered was giving Jonathan the finger as I pulled onto 11th, leaving him to find his own way home.

No.

The last thing I remembered was hearing a horn blaring in my ear and turning to see a tanker truck bearing down on the passenger side of the car.

A girl wandered into the kitchen wearing pajamas covered with yellow butterflies. She looked to be about six. Or four. Maybe seven.

"Morning, pumpkin."

She frowned and sat at the far end of the table, pouring herself some cereal and milk.

Probably not four.

Only a moment later, two other kids stumbled into the kitchen, a boy about ten and another girl, maybe eight?

"Hey." I nodded a greeting.

I had a wife and three kids. God was real and I was in hell.

The boy and the older girl started fighting over one of the cereal boxes. "Stop it, Juniper!" the boy called out.

"You stop, Jaren! You finished the box last time."

"Juniper!"

Eternal damnation. Of all things for my dad to be right about.

"Jaren!"

"Oh. My. God," I said, and something in my tone made the kids stop and turn toward me. "Did your parents really name you that?"

Juniper pursed her lips just as her mother had a few hours earlier, and the two older children exchanged a look. The younger girl, Jamie, I supposed, seemed oblivious, fishing for one of the multi-colored globs floating in her bowl.

"Mrs. Howell said we should turn our parents in if they use drugs," Jaren announced, apropos of nothing.

"Mrs. Howell probably needs to get laid," I told him.

All three kids stared at me, though they were too young to understand what I'd said. My subconscious was making them more sophisticated than real kids.

But this all *felt* real. What if some metaphysical something-or-other had done this? No one in their right mind would believe me. I'd be locked up and put in a straitjacket.

I was Jennifer Love Hewitt explaining to someone in every episode of *Ghost Whisperer* why they needed to believe the unbelievable.

Only the person I needed to convince of the truth was *me*.

My heart began beating faster and a drop of sweat trickled down my left temple. I heard footsteps approaching and wondered how I was going to keep up this charade. Perhaps it didn't matter if the woman called someone to cart me off to an institution. I was clearly delusional.

But first, goddammit, I was going to have a meal with my family.

I'd always eaten breakfast alone growing up, even when my parents were at the table. They'd have bacon and eggs, maybe some buttered toast, while I was handed an off-brand Pop-Tart. It wasn't that Mom was negligent. She genuinely believed I preferred the dry pastry.

I think.

Dinner, though, that was different. Mom always prepared enough of the good stuff—roast beef with carrots and potatoes, steak and corn on the cob—while also preparing punishment food, usually a can of potted meat, just for me in case she or Dad caught me doing something unmanly before dinner.

Like reading a book. Or listening to the Backstreet Boys.

"Good morning!" my wife said in a faux cheerful tone as she walked into the kitchen. Her half-closed eyelids suggested the shower hadn't been as successful as she'd hoped, but she was still alert enough to see that Jaren and Juniper were both clutching the same box.

"If there's not enough," the woman said, "just mix in some other cereal. It'll make a new flavor. Be adventurous. It's the only way to get ahead in life."

Jaren groaned and released his hold on the box. Juniper ripped it away victoriously and poured the last of the contents into her bowl, so much there was hardly any room left for milk.

The woman began asking the kids what their upcoming day at school looked like, and I retreated from the conversation. I could hardly start calling her "Mother" like a dad in a 1950s sit-com. Perhaps when everyone was gone, I'd have a chance to find some addressed mail, a passport maybe. Look up the news online to see what day it was. Call someone.

Not Jonathan.

Jamie sneezed, spraying the table with milk.

"Gross!" Jaren shouted.

"You're such a baby," Juniper told her sister.

"Be nice," the woman said, grabbing a paper towel from the counter and wiping Jamie's face and then the table. "She's sick. Your dad'll be staying home to watch her."

Damn. How long was this dream going to last?

I knew it wasn't a dream.

Or it was and it wasn't, like Captain Picard's experience in "The Inner Light," when he witnesses the last days of a world whose sun is dying.

Jamie didn't even seem all that sick. Probably just trying to get out of school.

Or kindergarten. I still didn't know how old she was.

Even if I hadn't been gay, I wouldn't have had any kids. No way I was wasting my youth and my money and my (natural!) testosterone worrying about someone else's future. I had my own now to concentrate on—Halloween in San Francisco, Mardi Gras in Sydney, Southern Decadence in New Orleans.

"Won't you, Nick?" I heard someone say and slowly began noticing again the other people at the table.

I looked at the woman sitting across from me.

"Won't you?" she repeated.

"Um…"

"You will look up some more memory exercises we can try tonight?" she asked.

"Absolutely," I said.

The woman smiled and gave me a wink.

Perhaps this was only Purgatory.

Soon, breakfast was over, the woman was out the door on her way to work, and I still didn't know her name. Jaren and Jupiter followed soon after, heading to the corner where the school bus would pick them up. We were apparently in suburbia.

Hell. Definitely hell.

I was about to turn on the TV when Jamie held up a hand. "Mom'll be mad if you don't put the dishes in the dishwasher."

Surely, whatever this was couldn't drag through the whole day, but just in case, I did as Jamie directed while she sat at the table and observed. She didn't cough or sneeze once.

"Are you really sick?" I asked. "Or was someone mean to you at school?"

Uh-oh. I forgot I didn't know if she was even in school yet.

The girl remained silent, and I was afraid I'd been caught.

"Jamie?"

"Mrs. Forster keeps making me stand in the corner with my nose against the wall."

"Excuse me?" I stopped and turned to look at her. What *year* was this, anyway? The kitchen appliances looked reasonably contemporary. "Whatever for?"

Jamie shrugged. "I don't think she likes when people have more than two kids."

My mouth fell open.

"I'll have a talk with Mrs. Forster," I said.

I wouldn't really. I wouldn't be here that long. But the promise needed to be made.

Then again, what did I care about this girl I didn't even know? I closed my eyes.

It wasn't *fair* for adults to ruin a child's life.

"What would you like to do today, pumpkin?"

We watched a couple of movies. *Encanto* and *Up.* When Jamie fell asleep on the sofa next to me, I brushed the hair off her forehead and realized she did feel warm. Maybe she *was* sick.

I turned the volume down on the TV and switched to cable to watch some news and get my bearings. The local channels seemed to be centered in Denver.

I'd never bothered to visit this town before.

The Antarctic was 70 degrees warmer than usual for this time of year, the Arctic 60 degrees warmer. A car bomb had exploded in Afghanistan. Lawmakers in Idaho were trying to put parents of trans kids in prison. Oil prices in the U.S. were lower this week but gas prices were higher. Thirteen people had drowned in a subway in China.

My head hurt. I touched the back of my head and winced.

Everyone had seen enough science fiction shows to "believe" weird crap was possible. *Stranger Things*, *Quantum Leap*, *Dr. Who*. No one believed a fairy tale like "Jack and the Beanstalk," but some of these other scenarios we kept in the part of our brain reserved for "Not really but maybe. Who knows? Why not? No way."

Perhaps I'd ruptured a blood vessel in that part of my brain and damaged it.

A loud honking screech blared out of the television in repeated bursts. Jamie stirred beside me and slowly sat up. A newscaster appeared off to one side of the screen while the other two thirds showed an aerial view of a massive wildfire sweeping toward a street lined with new construction. A few of the buildings looked freshly completed, with new sod in rectangles and signs posted near the sidewalk. Smoke billowed high into the air.

Three tiny figures ran out of one of the finished houses, the camera zooming in while one of the figures jumped into a car. Jamie stiffened beside me.

"That's Mom!" she shouted.

I honestly couldn't recognize the figure in all the commotion, and I hadn't watched this morning to see what she was driving. Jamie was probably just assuming the worst. It certainly didn't look good for whoever those people were. Some of the new construction was now burning, the flames jumping and spreading fast. Smoke crossed the road in both directions. We watched as the woman took off and disappeared into the blackness. The roof of the house she'd exited only moments before caught fire.

"Officials have issued an evacuation order for residents on the west side of Superior. The wildfire is heading toward the McCaslin Boulevard/Coalton Road area."

"Is that anywhere near us, pumpkin?" I asked quietly.

Jamie looked up at me and shrugged, turning back to stare at the images on the television. I stood and nonchalantly headed to the kitchen for a glass of water, really searching for a cell phone. Jamie's mother would have hers with her, so anything left here would be Nick's.

Yep, there it was, recharging on the counter. I picked it up and turned it on.

Locked.

But it used facial recognition, thank God, and not a pin.

I casually looked out the front window to read the address on the house across the street.

"What street do we live on, pumpkin?" No way to ask that without sounding like an idiot, but I could see smoke from here. It didn't look far away.

This was a suburb, for God's sake, not some rural mining town in the mountains. Folks from the three houses

I could see through our front window were throwing a few things into their cars and taking off.

I scrolled through Nick's contacts but didn't know which of the female names was his wife's.

Why wasn't *she* calling?

"They're evacuating the schools!" Jamie squealed from the sofa. "Daddy! What's going to happen to Juniper and Jaren?"

What kind of hell had I found myself in?

"What's the name of your school?" I asked. All three kids must still attend the same one.

"John Moore." She stood in front of the television, leaning forward and staring.

I couldn't find a school with that name but tried "Jon" instead. Nothing. Then "John M." And suddenly "John Muir" popped up. "You know how to get there from here, pumpkin?"

Jamie shook her head. I'd use GPS.

"Get dressed," I said quietly. "We're going to get your brother and sister." I tried to figure out where Nick might keep his keys and found them next to his wallet in a little nook near the entrance to the laundry room.

There were shouts outside, the sound of tires squealing. By the time we pulled onto the street, traffic was thick but moving.

Too bad this guy didn't have a faster car. It didn't *have* to be a Lamborghini. An Alfa Romeo would do.

"In 500 feet, turn left," a voice on Nick's phone told me. Almost half the sky was black, and the voice was leading me toward the worst of it.

Would it be wrong to just drive away? Even if this was all a bad dream, I'd heard that if you died in your dream, you really did die. Of course, how could there ever have been a study to prove that?

It took almost ten minutes on the increasingly clogged roads to approach the school. Two dozen cars were lined up in front, with parents standing beside open doors and waving at the crowds streaming from the building. A few buses were in the school bus driveway and teachers and staff were running toward their cars in the parking lot.

Several of the teachers ushered small children to hurry along with them. Two middle-aged women wearing orange vests over their regular clothing pushed kids into buses. A handful of parents found their kids and floored their gas pedals getting away.

It was a miracle no one was run over.

There was no such thing as miracles.

"Jaren!" Jamie called out her window. "Juniper!" No one could possibly hear in the midst of all the shouting and yelling and crackling and creaking and groaning. The wind had picked up and roared all around us. Hot embers flew high overhead.

Could I even remember what the kids looked like? I'd only seen them a few minutes this morning.

I looked over my shoulder and saw several homes burning a block back. Up ahead, a single home was ablaze.

The roof of the gymnasium caught fire. Parents honked their horns and screamed.

"Makisha!"

"Terry!"

"Christopher!"

"Baran!"

Every year, I heard about things like this. Paradise going up in flames. Lytton. Pine City. Gatlinburg. All places no one important lived. And those people knew what risks they were taking when they moved there. Like the idiots who lived in basement apartments that got flooded. Like the morons who lived in avalanche country.

I stepped out of my car. "Just grab a kid and go!" I shouted. But parents wouldn't leave without their own.

What, after all, did I understand about family ties? I didn't even send my mom Christmas cards.

She didn't send me any, either.

I needed to leave with Jamie before we both died. But only a moment later another man shouted from the car behind me. "Fill your car with whatever kids you can and we'll get yours!"

A mother in front repeated the call, and soon we formed a bucket brigade, people tossing random children into cars and screeching off.

Homes were burning all around us. The main school building erupted into flames. Kids still wearing heavy backpacks began running down the street, no longer waiting for vehicles. The last school bus was near the end of the block. What looked like a young boy hanging onto the door fell into the street.

This couldn't be happening, I told myself for the thousandth time today, pushing a kid into the front seat of Nick's car. This couldn't be happening. How could this be happening? I just wanted to go back to my condo in Chelsea. Kick back with some weed and watch a fun movie. *The Hunger Games. The Day After Tomorrow.*

Jonathan had looked a bit like Jake Gyllenhaal.

Was he a witch? A demon? A devil? Who had put me in this nightmare of a life?

Maybe I was in a coma.

The heat was blistering. I could feel my eyes drying out. Tiny embers no larger than grains of sand pelted us like burning needles.

Jamie screamed.

I grabbed four more kids and crammed them in the back seat next to my daughter, slamming my door and pulling away. The smoke was now so dense I couldn't be sure I wasn't about to run over some other kid. I could see flames on both sides of the street, glowing through the thickening smoke.

"Don't let me die, Daddy!" Jamie shouted, her voice muffled as she shrunk onto the floor. I hoped her mother, whatever her name, was okay. The other kids breathed heavily but said nothing.

The car in front of me stopped, engulfed in flames. Two people staggered out, burning, and collapsed.

"Everyone down!" I shouted.

There were no atheists in foxholes, I remembered, but I still didn't believe in God. What kind of god would allow such a massacre?

And I was no savior, that was for sure.

In the rearview mirror, I saw the street behind me explode into flames. I steered to the side of the car blocking me, ran over a burning, writhing body, and gunned the engine, driving as fast as I could into more of the thick black smoke.

What Readers Have Said

Townsend's stories are "a gay *Portnoy's Complaint* of Mormonism. Salacious, sweet, sad, insightful, insulting, religiously ethnic, quirky-faithful, and funny."

D. Michael Quinn, author of *The Mormon Hierarchy: Origins of Power*

"Told from a believably conversational first-person perspective, [*The Abominable Gayman*'s] novelistic focus on Anderson's journey to thoughtful self-acceptance allows for greater character development than often seen in short stories, which makes this well-paced work rich and satisfying, and one of Townsend's strongest. An extremely important contribution to the field of Mormon fiction." Named to Kirkus Reviews' Best of 2011.

Kirkus Reviews

"The thirteen stories in *Mormon Underwear* capture this struggle [between Mormonism and homosexuality] with humor, sadness, insight, and sometimes shocking details....*Mormon Underwear* provides compelling stories, literally from the inside-out."

Niki D'Andrea, *Phoenix New Times*

"Townsend's lively writing style and engaging characters [in *Zombies for Jesus*] make for stories which force us to wake up, smell the (prohibited) coffee, and review our attitudes with regard to reading dogma so doggedly. These are tales which revel in the individual tics and quirks which make us human, Mormon or not, gay or not…"

A.J. Kirby, *The Short Review*

"The Rift," from *The Abominable Gayman*, is a "fascinating tale of an untenable situation…a *tour de force*."

David Lenson, editor, *The Massachusetts Review*

"Pronouncing the Apostrophe," from *The Golem of Rabbi Loew*, is "quiet and revealing, an intriguing tale…"

Sima Rabinowitz, Literary Magazine Review, *NewPages.com*

The Circumcision of God is "a collection of short stories that consider the imperfect, silenced majority of Mormons, who may in fact be [the Church's] best hope….[The book leaves] readers regretting the church's willingness to marginalize those who best exemplify its ideals: those who love fiercely despite all obstacles, who brave challenges at great personal risk and who always choose the hard, higher road."

Kirkus Reviews

In *Mormon Fairy Tales*, Johnny Townsend displays "both a wicked sense of irony and a deep well of compassion."

Kel Munger, *Sacramento News and Review*

Zombies for Jesus is "eerie, erotic, and magical."

Publishers Weekly

"While [Townsend's] many touching vignettes draw deeply from Mormon mythology, history, spirituality and culture, [*Mormon Fairy Tales*] is neither a gaudy act of proselytism nor angry protest literature from an ex-believer. Like all good fiction, his stories are simply about the joys, the hopes and the sorrows of people."

Kirkus Reviews

"In *Let the Faggots Burn* author Johnny Townsend restores this tragic event [the UpStairs Lounge fire] to its proper place in LGBT history and reminds us that the victims of the blaze were not just 'statistics,' but real people with real lives, families, and friends."

Jesse Monteagudo, *The Bilerico Project*

In *Let the Faggots Burn,* "Townsend's heart-rending descriptions of the victims…seem to [make them] come alive once more."

Kit Van Cleave, *OutSmart Magazine*

Marginal Mormons is "an irreverent, honest look at life outside the mainstream Mormon Church….Throughout his musings on sin and forgiveness, Townsend beautifully demonstrates his characters' internal, perhaps irreconcilable struggles….Rather than anger and disdain, he offers an honest portrayal of people searching for meaning and community in their lives, regardless of their life choices or secrets." Named to Kirkus Reviews' Best of 2012.

Kirkus Reviews

The stories in *The Mormon Victorian Society* "register the new openness and confidence of gay life in the age of same-sex marriage….What hasn't changed is Townsend's wry, conversational prose, his subtle evocations of character and social dynamics, and his deadpan humor. His warm empathy still glows in this intimate yet clear-eyed engagement with Mormon theology and folkways. Funny, shrewd and finely wrought dissections of the awkward contradictions—and surprising harmonies—between conscience and desire." Named to Kirkus Reviews' Best of 2013.

Kirkus Reviews

"This collection of short stories [*The Mormon Victorian Society*] featuring gay Mormon characters slammed [me] in the face from the first page, wrestled my heart and mind to the floor, and left me panting and wanting more by the end. Johnny Townsend has created so many memorable characters in such few pages. I went weeks thinking about this book. It truly touched me."

Tom Webb, *A Bear on Books*

Dragons of the Book of Mormon is an "entertaining collection....Townsend's prose is sharp, clear, and easy to read, and his characters are well rendered..."

Publishers Weekly

"The pre-eminent documenter of alternative Mormon lifestyles...Townsend has a deep understanding of his characters, and his limpid prose, dry humor and well-grounded (occasionally magical) realism make their spiritual conundrums both compelling and entertaining. [*Dragons of the Book of Mormon* is] [a]nother of Townsend's critical but affectionate and absorbing tours of Mormon discontent." Named to Kirkus Reviews' Best of 2014.

Kirkus Reviews

In *Gayrabian Nights*, "Townsend's prose is always limpid and evocative, and…he finds real drama and emotional depth in the most ordinary of lives."

Kirkus Reviews

Gayrabian Nights is a "complex revelation of how seriously soul damaging the denial of the true self can be."

Ryan Rhodes, author of *Free Electricity*

Gayrabian Nights "was easily the most original book I've read all year. Funny, touching, topical, and thoroughly enjoyable."

Rainbow Awards

Lying for the Lord is "one of the most gripping books that I've picked up for quite a while. I love the author's writing style, alternately cynical, humorous, biting, scathing, poignant, and touching…. This is the third book of his that I've read, and all are equally engaging. These are stories that need to be told, and the author does it in just the right way."

Heidi Alsop, *Ex-Mormon Foundation Board Member*

In *Lying for the Lord*, Townsend "gets under the skin of his characters to reveal their complexity and conflicts….shrewd, evocative [and] wryly humorous."

Kirkus Reviews

In *Missionaries Make the Best Companions*, "the author treats the clash between religious dogma and liberal humanism with vivid realism, sly humor, and subtle feeling as his characters try to figure out their true missions in life. Another of Townsend's rich dissections of Mormon failures and uncertainties…" Named to Kirkus Reviews' Best of 2015.

Kirkus Reviews

In *Invasion of the Spirit Snatchers*, "Townsend, a confident and practiced storyteller, skewers the hypocrisies and eccentricities of his characters with precision and affection. The outlandish framing narrative is the most consistent source of shock and humor, but the stories do much to ground the reader in the world—or former world—of the characters….A funny, charming tale about a group of Mormons facing the end of the world."

Kirkus Reviews

"Townsend's collection [*The Washing of Brains*] once again displays his limpid, naturalistic prose, skillful narrative chops, and his subtle insights into psychology…Well-crafted dispatches on the clash between religion and self-fulfillment…"

Kirkus Reviews

"While the author is generally at his best when working as a satirist, there are some fine, understated touches in these tales [*The Last Days Linger*] that will likely affect readers in subtle ways....readers should come away impressed by the deep empathy he shows for all his characters—even the homophobic ones."

Kirkus Reviews

"Written in a conversational style that often uses stories and personal anecdotes to reveal larger truths, this immensely approachable book [*Racism by Proxy*] skillfully serves its intended audience of White readers grappling with complex questions regarding race, history, and identity. The author's frequent references to the Church of Jesus Christ of Latter-day Saints may be too niche for readers unfamiliar with its idiosyncrasies, but Townsend generally strikes a perfect balance of humor, introspection, and reasoned arguments that will engage even skeptical readers."

Kirkus Reviews

Orgy at the STD Clinic portrays "an all-too real scenario that Townsend skewers to wincingly accurate proportions...[with] instant classic moments courtesy of his punchy, sassy, sexy lead character..."

Jim Piechota, *Bay Area Reporter*

Orgy at the STD Clinic is "…a triumph of humane sensibility. A richly textured saga that brilliantly captures the fraying social fabric of contemporary life." Named to Kirkus Reviews' Best Indie Books of 2022.

Kirkus Reviews

Ingram Content Group UK Ltd.
Milton Keynes UK
UKHW011943080523
421401UK00004B/384